MARKED FOR DANGER

MARK

ANNA BLAKELY

Marked for Danger

Marked Series 5

First Edition
Copyright © 2023 Saje Publishing
All rights reserved.
All cover art and logo Copyright © 2022
Publisher: Saje Publishing
Cover by: Lori Jackson

All rights reserved. No part of this book may be reproduced in any form or by any electronic or mechanical means, including information storage and retrieval systems—except in the case of brief quotations embodied in critical articles or reviews—without permission in writing from the author.
This book is a work of fiction. The names, characters, and places portrayed in this book are entirely products of the author's imagination or used fictitiously. Any resemblance to actual events, locales, or persons, living or dead, is entirely coincidental and not intended by the author.
The unauthorized reproduction or distribution of this copyrighted work is illegal. Criminal copyright infringement, including infringement without monetary gain, is investigated by the FBI and is punishable by up to five years in federal prison and a fine of $250,000.00.
If you find any eBooks being sold or shared illegally, please contact the author at anna@annablakelycom.

❦ Created with Vellum

ABOUT THE BOOK

A detective with a big heart and a deadly aim. A psychologist whose loyalty could get her killed. A ruthless criminal willing to do whatever it takes to get what he wants.

Denver Detective Grady Thorne has found a new home in the DPD. He has a partner he trusts, a unit he respects, and a boss he admires. Then there's Izzy. Smart, sexy, and willing to keep things casual, the mouthwatering psychiatrist's no-strings arrangement is all Grady needs. Or so he thinks. But this reluctant detective is about to realize just how far he'll go for the woman threatening to break through his long-standing defenses.

Dr. Isobel "Izzy" Garcia knows what it's like to be failed by the system. Her broken past is also why she refuses to let anyone get too close...especially the sexy-as-sin Detective Thorne. Until now, their secret friends-with-benefits agreement has given her everything she needs. But when Izzy and her estranged brother find themselves in the crosshairs of a killer, she'll do whatever it takes to protect the only family she has left. Even if it means putting her life—and heart—in Grady's hands.

With danger knocking on Izzy's door, Grady vows to keep her safe. But time is running out, and if they can't find the person behind the attacks on her life in time, it'll be too late for them all. Because the man they're after is driven by a deep-seated revenge, and he won't stop until Izzy's guarded heart stops beating…forever.

Marked for Danger is Book 5 in the bestselling **Marked Series. Filled with excitement, heart-racing intrigue, and a steamy, once-in-a-lifetime love, this friends-turned-lovers romantic suspense novel is sure to keep you on the edge of your seat from the first page to the last. With appearances from all your favorite Marked characters, Grady and Izzy's story promises readers a happy ever after with no cliffhangers.

To those who serve.

PROLOGUE

Sitting propped up on a gurney in the back of the ambulance, legs stretched out in front of her beneath a thin white blanket, fifteen-year-old Izzy Garcia's tear-filled gaze took in the scene through the emergency vehicle's opened back doors. Her hazel eyes followed the young man being placed in the back of a police car, her heart giving a breath-stealing thump when he turned his head in her direction.

A line of shivers raced down Izzy's spine, the chill not created by a passing breeze but rather the young man's cold, accepting gaze. With his hands cuffed, nose bloodied, and his hair a disheveled mess, there wasn't a stitch of regret to be found.

Not that she'd expected there to be.

"What's going to happen to him?" The question sounded flat, even to her.

The kind detective sitting on the tiny built-in bench to her left followed Izzy's line of sight. "Tonight?" She shrugged. "He'll be booked, processed, and placed in a cell until his arraignment."

"And then?" She needed to know.

"Then it's up to the judge. But the charges against him are serious."

Breaking and entering, assault, attempted murder...yes, she supposed those were some serious charges.

Hugging herself, Izzy ignored her throbbing jaw and rubbed her sore wrists. Like the inside of her right thigh—where she'd been repeatedly punched in order to spread her legs open—the skin there was already starting to bruise.

"When will he get out?" A tear fell down her tender cheek.

"Depends on how good his lawyer is. I know it's hard but try not to think about that, okay?" The pretty redhead put a cautious hand on Izzy's shoulder. "All you need to worry about right now is letting these guys take care of you and getting some rest."

Rest.

Izzy nearly choked at the thought. She'd been knocked around and nearly raped less than an hour ago, and she was expected to just forget all that and what...take a nap? Not likely.

"Where will I go?" More tears fell as she watched the police cruiser drive away.

But before the detective could answer, the paramedic who'd initiated treatment reached out and pulled the back doors shut. Though it shouldn't have been, the sound of metal slamming together was deafening.

Frowning, Izzy looked to her left. She wanted to ask the nice female detective why it had sounded like that. Why she could still hear the vibrations rippling through the enclosed space. But the detective who'd been by her side from the moment she'd arrived was gone. And in her place...

No!

Izzy's heart flew into her throat, its heavy beats slamming against her insides with a force unlike any she'd ever felt before. Because the eyes staring back at her now belonged to him.

The person who'd come into her bedroom tonight. The man who'd put his hands on her, despite her repeated attempts to say no. Attempts stifled by a rough hand pressed against her lips.

Hand to her mouth. Heavy body on hers. Fist to her thigh. Another hand forcing her wrists between their bodies, the delicate bones there grinding painfully together as she fought to get free.

And when he'd realized the control was all his, that hand on her wrists had started to move lower. His unwanted fingers pulling at the elastic on the waist of her underwear. And then—

"No!" Izzy gasped, her entire upper body shooting straight up from the mattress below. Chest heaving with forceful, terror-fueled breaths, she broke up the heavy puffs of air with several hard, painful swallows.

Her lids closed and opened, the series of purposeful blinks slowly bringing her back to the present.

He's not here. It was only a dream.

Only it wasn't a dream. It was a memory. One Izzy had spent the last sixteen years trying to forget. But it was impossible to forget the very thing that had shaped her life every year—or rather, every month, week, day, hour, minute, and second—since.

Which reminded her...

She turned to the sleeping man lying beside her. Grady Thorne's smooth scalp was a stark contrast to the thick and neat salt-and-pepper beard covering his strong jaw and framing his relaxed lips.

Lips that were intimately familiar with nearly every inch of her five-eight frame.

Lost in a sea of slumber, the sexy detective's broad, muscular chest rose and fell with slow, even breaths. His expression was that of peace, despite the dangers and evil she knew he encountered on a regular basis.

And though their...*arrangement*...was purely casual, his mere presence always made her feel safe.

Safe. I'm here with Grady, and I'm safe.

Warmth spread across her chest as the stolen moment

gave way to wishful thinking. Before Izzy knew it, her mind became filled with all sorts of wistful, wondering questions and thoughts.

Things like, what would it be like to fall asleep next to the sexy detective every night? Or to wake up to his entrancing blue gaze and dimpled cheeks every morning?

Adjusting the sheet covering her naked body, she imagined what it would be like to sit side-by-side on his balcony, sipping coffee as the morning sun filled their gazes. And the most shocking of wonders, Izzy found herself not only thinking about what her life would look like if it were permanently intertwined with Grady's...but also wishing it was.

What the hell?

Shocked by the unexpected thought, she hurriedly slid across the mattress, putting as much distance between them as she could without toppling off the bed. The rustling of Grady's dark blue bedding filled the otherwise silent space, the tips of Izzy's dark hair tickling her bare neck with a sharp shake of her head.

The move transported her back from a land of make believe and into the real world where she belonged.

What are you doing?

Izzy studied Grady's handsome, oblivious face. Her gut tightened with guilt, her heart and mind fully aware that a man like him deserved more. Not that he wanted it. Not yet. But experience had taught her he would.

They always did. More time. More trust. More commitment. More...

Me.

It was the one thing Izzy couldn't give, and the one rule she had when it came to her lovers. No strings. No emotions. Not ever.

Yet here she was, spending the night with Grady. Again.

She didn't usually sleep over after their private trysts. Sex was one thing, but spending the entire night together was too personal. Too risky. Yet this was the third time she'd fallen asleep in the safety and comfort of the sexy detective's warm embrace.

The first two times, she'd managed to wake up well before sunrise, leaving a quick note using an early workday as an excuse. Today, however...

Izzy glanced to her right, her chest tightening when she took in the floor-to-ceiling windows lining the exposed brick wall to her right and frowned. The rising sun taunted her from behind the folded blinds, a reminder that she was getting far too comfortable when it came to Grady.

The psychiatrist in her was fully aware of how backward her outlook on romantic relationships was. But her education and training had also provided an explanation for her inability to let *anyone* get too close.

Not that she needed it spelled out for her.

Unfortunately Izzy knew precisely why she always kept the men in her life at a distance. Why, despite her most recent thoughts, she'd allowed the man still sleeping beside her to touch her body...but not her heart.

And no matter how much she wished things could be different—no matter what she did to fight against it, the perpetual cycle was never-ending. Which was why she didn't even bother trying to fight it anymore.

It is what it is, Iz.

The pressure in Izzy's chest grew as the decades-old silent phrase rolled through her mind. It was something her father—and then later, her older brother—would always say. Their way of making her see a given situation for what it was and accept facts when there wasn't anything she could do to change it.

And since she'd long ago given up on trying to change who she was...

Izzy lowered her gaze to Grady once more. She waited, holding her breath while she counted a handful of his before slowly and carefully slipping out from beneath the covers.

Padding barefoot—and bare-assed—across his wide-open loft apartment's wooden floor, she did her best to keep her steps silent, stopping every few steps to gather her discarded clothing from the night before. As usual, the evidence of their explosive passion had resulted in a trail running from the door to his bed.

A particularly arousing memory flashed in her mind's eye as Izzy set the haphazard pile down onto Grady's butcher block island countertop. Dressing in haste, the erotic replay filled her thoughts, frame by heart-racing frame.

Grady's mouth on hers. Strong hands ripping off her clothes and then gripping her hips as he took her against his living room wall. Muscular, tatted arms holding her close. The slight smattering of hair on his chest creating a tantalizing friction against her breasts as he carried her across the open space to his king-sized bed.

By the time the memory had dissipated, Izzy's cheeks were flushed, and her body ached for more.

She looked back at the bed, more than a little tempted to return to its soft warmth—and the unmoving man still sleeping beneath its covers. Lately, her usual morning-after move had become harder and harder to bear.

Though part of her—a *big* part—wanted nothing more than to stay in Grady's bed forever, Izzy knew it was an impossible dream. She also recognized the signs that it was time to move on.

You've already stayed too long, Iz. It's time to go.

An invisible fist squeezed her heart, a sudden stinging forming in the corners of her eyes. Because that voice in her head wasn't merely referring to the past few hours.

Normally ending things was a non-issue since she made it very clear from the beginning with any man she became intimately involved with. And it wasn't like she hopped from bed to bed. Quite the opposite, actually.

Izzy was very, *very* particular about who she chose as a sexual partner. In fact, at the ripe old age of thirty-one, she still only needed one hand to count the number of men she'd slept with. And when those no-strings relationships had ended, both participants walked away without a single drop of animosity or remorse.

But something about this time, this *man*, was different.

The slight sound of sheets rustling pulled Izzy from her thoughts, her focus returning to the bed in time to see a still-sleeping Grady roll from his back to his side. Her stomach clenched as an unfamiliar feeling began to settle deep inside, and it took her a few seconds to realize what it was.

Regret.

For the first time in her life, Izzy regretted the casual relationship she was about to sever. Not because she was worried about upsetting Grady. The whole no-strings arrangement had been his idea from the start.

No, the regret she felt was purely selfish. These last few months with the mouthwatering detective had been fun. Exciting, even. And the sex…

He makes me feel things I've never felt before.

It was another reason to get out now, before someone

got hurt. And Izzy had a feeling if she continued seeing Grady outside the occasional, professional interaction at work, *she* would be the one left bearing the scars.

She turned away, slipping her purse's thin leather strap over one shoulder. With her keys and a pair of shiny red heels dangling from one hand, Izzy used the small notepad and pen Grady kept by his landline phone to scribble one final note...

Early day in court. Thanks for last night!
~Izzy

That was it. No "see you at work" or "call me". Definitely no, "I'll call you." Because she wouldn't be calling him. Not unless it was work related.

Not anymore.

Izzy drew in a stuttered breath as she placed the pen neatly beside the impersonal note. With a sigh, she allowed herself a final glimpse of what she wished could continue but knew had to end.

Committing the image of Grady's peaceful, sexy, sleeping form to memory before carefully unlocking and opening his door...shutting it silently behind her.

Though the decision to do so was a necessary evil—just as it had the other times she'd ended things with the other men from her past—Izzy couldn't help but acknowledge this time felt different.

And as she slipped her feet into her heels and headed for her car, she ignored the nagging feeling that this time —*this* time—she was making a huge mistake.

1

"Dr. Garcia, in your professional opinion, do you feel this court should award Mr. Shipman full custody of his son at this time?" ADA Angelia Roussos—Denver's lead family court prosecutor—stood in front of Izzy and waited.

As the DPD's new forensic psychiatrist, Izzy's duties varied depending upon the department's needs. Things like going to fresh crime scenes to offer her professional opinion about the victims and/or killers, working with the local FBI office when a criminal profile was needed, assisting SWAT with hostage negotiations, and most often, offering an unbiased professional opinion as an expert witness for the DPD and the state of Colorado.

Typically the cases for which she testified were criminal, but Izzy also worked closely with the D.A.'s office during the more serious family court proceedings. Like this one.

Turning away from ADA Roussos—a woman Izzy had a fairly solid working relationship with—Izzy looked directly at the judge when she answered Angelia's question with a firm and concise, "No. I do not believe Mr. Shipman should be awarded custody of his son."

Though the graying woman sitting behind the bench couldn't say it without causing a mistrial, the look in the judge's wise eyes told Izzy everything she needed to know.

She agrees with me.

"Dr. Garcia," ADA Roussos continued. "Can you please explain to the court what brought you to this conclusion?" The tips of her sandy blonde, shoulder-length hair brushed against her gray suit jacket's lapel as she moved.

From her place on the witness stand, Izzy kept her spine straight and her eyes on her colleague as she answered with, "I met with Mr. Shipman earlier this week."

"What did the two of you discuss?"

"Mr. Shipman and I spoke of the events leading to his prior assault and battery arrest, his conviction, and subsequent incarceration. We also talked about the therapy sessions he attended while in prison, as well as his plans moving forward, should the court grant him partial or full custody of his minor child."

"And did the plaintiff share with you any details regarding how he planned to care for his son?"

"He did." Izzy nodded.

"Can you please share with the court what those plans include?"

A whole lot of bullshit, but I can't exactly say that on the record now, can I?

"Mr. Shipman told me he's been renting a small apartment across town, and he's been working a part-time job at a local grocery store a few blocks from where he lives. He told me he recently purchased a used vehicle that, according to him, is reliable enough to get him back and forth to work, as well as driving his son to and from school."

ADA Roussos's big blue eyes grew wide as she slid her surprised gaze from Izzy to the judge, and back again.

"Sounds to me like Mr. Shipman is ready and willing to provide a stable home environment for both him and his son."

"On paper, yes." Izzy nodded. "I'd have to agree."

The intelligent attorney frowned. "I apologize, Dr. Garcia, but...I'm a little confused. You just testified to the plaintiff having a good, solid plan on how he will care and provide for his young son, yet seconds before, you told this court it's your professional opinion that custody should *not* be awarded to Mr. Shipman. Can you please explain why that is?"

Izzy did look at the man in question, then. With his receding, nearly bald on top hairline, deep crow's feet and cold demeanor, Todd Shipman appeared much older than his thirty-eight years. The man was a felon who'd been granted an early release from his five-year prison sentence for assault and battery against his now-deceased ex-wife.

From the information Izzy had been provided by the D.A.'s office, the former Mrs. Shipman had become a slave to painkillers and alcohol—a result of her endless search to escape the depression and anguish Shipman's physical and mental abuse had created. Unfortunately the poor woman died of an accidental overdose eight months ago, leaving Michael—the couple's six-year-old son—in the hands of Child Protective Services.

Now that he'd been let out early due to prison overcrowding, Todd Shipman wanted full custody of Michael. Something Izzy desperately wanted to keep from happening.

"During my session with the plaintiff, Mr. Shipman exhibited numerous behavioral characteristics consistent with NPD, or narcissistic personality disorder. This disorder is comprised of a pervasive pattern of grandiosity, including but not limited to a constant need for attention and admiration, as well as an inflated sense of self-importance. In addition to this, Mr. Shipman also showed signs of having a grandiose sense of self-importance."

"Meaning?"

"In layman's terms, it basically means he thinks he's smarter and more important than those around him."

"Objection." Shipman's attorney stood from his seat and faced the judge. "Dr. Garcia can't possibly know what my client thinks about himself or anyone else."

"That's quite literally her job, Your Honor," ADA Roussos was quick to rebut. "Dr. Garcia isn't a friend or neighbor who's been called to the stand as a character witness. She's the state's expert witness, and her professional opinion of Mr. Shipman's personality and behavior are extremely relevant and must be taken into consideration before a judgement can be made on this case."

"I agree with Ms. Roussos." Judge Hamlin nodded. "Your objection is overruled, Mr. Browning. Ms. Roussos, you may continue."

"Thank you, Your Honor." To Izzy, Roussos added, "Please continue."

Izzy gave her a slight nod. "As I was saying, during our session, Mr. Shipman's main focus was himself, rather than his child. In the first few minutes, he did go over the steps he'd taken these last few months to ensure Michael had a stable and safe environment to grow up in, however the focus quickly shifted back to Mr. Shipman's belief that he was wrongfully convicted despite the overwhelming evidence to the contrary. When asked about the four documented physical altercations he was directly involved in while in prison, Mr. Shipman put the blame for each of those incidents onto the other inmates involved."

"He didn't take any responsibility for being a part of those fist fights?"

"No." Izzy shook her head. "Instead, he accused the guards on duty of setting him up."

"Were the guards in question the same ones working during the different brawls?"

Another negative shake. "They were not. According to the prison's employee logs, the guards were different during each of the altercations."

I checked.

"What else makes you believe Mr. Shipman should not be awarded custody of Michael?"

Izzy glanced to the plaintiff's table, the man's cold angry stare presumably meant to intimidate. She refused to let it.

Over the next few minutes, those present listened as she gave several professionally detailed and medically sound explanations. Mr. Browning objected numerous times during her testimony, but thankfully Judge Hamlin saw through the man's desperation and overruled every Hail Mary attempt Browning threw at her.

When ADA Roussos had no further questions, Browning began his cross-examination. The slimy S.O.B. attempted to discredit Izzy's claims, doing his damnedest to twist and turn her words into something they weren't. Despite his efforts to make his client out to be the victim, Izzy kept her presence calm and professional, refusing to waver in her previous statements.

It wasn't hard to remain steadfast, however. Mainly because everything she'd said about Todd Shipman was true.

He was a narcissistic asshole who preyed on those he viewed as weak, including women and children. And—in Izzy's personal and professional opinion—the man's pursuit of custody didn't stem from a father's love, but rather the welfare checks and tax benefits being a single parent would provide.

In short, Shipman was trying to use his son for financial gain.

"I have no further questions for this witness, Your Honor."

With an offer of the court's thanks, Judge Hamlin gave Izzy permission to leave the stand. Rising to her feet, she carefully stepped down, her heels clicking across the shiny tiled floor as she moved. Keeping her shoulders back and her eyes forward, Izzy didn't give Todd Shipman the satisfaction of glancing his way as she walked past.

Seven minutes later, she'd made the two-block walk down West 14th Street to the parking garage located at 14th and Elati. Spotting her blue metallic Toyota 4Runner a few cars away, she worked her toned legs up the covered concrete incline.

When she was only two parking spots away from her SUV, Izzy released the gold clasp on the front of her black quilted shoulder bag and pulled out her keys. Pressing the fob's rubber unlock button, her movement faltered when a set of soft footfalls sounded from somewhere nearby.

She turned around but saw no one. Silently chiding herself for being paranoid—parking garages always gave her the creeps—Izzy continued on her current path. By the time she reached her 4Runner, she'd already moved on to her mental to-do list for the day.

Gym, check. Court, check. Go through the stack of new consult files on my desk... Yeah, that'll be checked off after a quick stop for a much-needed caffeine boost on my way to the precinct.

Izzy reached for her car door and pulled the handle.

Opening the door, she was about to climb inside when a deep, rumbly voice made her jump.

"Fancy meeting you here."

With an audible gasp, she spun on her heels to face the man standing inches away.

"Grady?" She put a hand over her racing heart and blew out a breath. "What the...you scared the *crap* out of me!"

"Sorry." He slid his large hands into his jeans pocket. With a smile that showed off his dimples, the infuriatingly sexy man looked as far away from sorry as was humanly possible.

Izzy pulled her lids together in a narrow gaze as she jutted her chin. "You did that on purpose."

"Maybe." A shrug of his broad shoulders. "I have a trial prep meeting with ADA Umbridge for next week's drug raid trial. I'd just parked down the hill when I saw you walking to your car. But I guess now we're even."

Her brows turned inward. "Even?"

"Sure. You snuck out on me this morning...*again*...so I snuck up on you. See?" Humor glittered in his hazel eyes. "Even."

"I didn't *sneak out* on you." Izzy became unnecessarily defensive. "I left you a note saying I had court early today."

"Oh, I got the note. Along with all the others you've left. You know, if we keep this up, it won't be long before I have enough to make my very own morning-after memoir."

The smile adorning his handsomely rugged face appeared genuine, but there was a sliver of a shadow hiding behind Grady's intelligent eyes. Izzy's gut tightened. Had her post-sex exits really hurt his feelings?

No, that couldn't be it. After all, hadn't *he* been the one to suggest their no-strings arrangement a few months earlier? Yes. Yes, he was.

And weren't you the one who'd snuck—ahem—left his apartment this morning having decided to break things off?

Damn her inner voice, anyway.

"Hey." Grady's forward movement pulled her attention back to the present. Concern pulled his brows together. "You okay? I was just playin' around."

"Were you?" She wanted to take back the words the second they were out.

The lines on his forehead smoothed as he straightened his spine. Standing inches above six feet, he seemed to tower over her. And if she hadn't hurt his feelings before...

"Yeah, Iz. I was."

Grady's assessing gaze made Izzy want to squirm. "I'm sorry." She sighed. "I didn't mean to be snippy."

"Bad day at court?" The concern returned to his tone.

"Actually, no. Court went very well." She adjusted the purse strap on her shoulder. "At least, I think it did. You never know for sure until the verdict comes down."

"This the custody case you told me about? That Shipman guy, right?"

Izzy nodded. "ADA Roussos argued a solid case, and I'm pretty sure Judge Hamlin was on the same page. Angelia said she'd let me know when Hamlin had reached her decision."

"Bet their expert witness sealed the deal." Grady winked with a sideways grin.

"Well from the way Todd Shipman stared me down when I got off the stand, I'd say he'd agree with you."

A sudden, almost fierce look stole his smile. "Did he threaten you? If he did, that's witness intimidation. Say the word, and I'll make sure—"

"No threats were made," she quickly informed him. "However, the man *does* have a mean stink-eye." Noticing the stiffness still very much present in Grady's tight neck and shoulders, Izzy instinctively put a palm to his chest and did her best to reassure him. "Relax, Grady. It was just a look. No need to go all alpha-protector on the jerk."

Secretly there was a part of Izzy that loved the man's protective streak.

One of his hands lifted to cover hers. His beating heart kicked hard beneath her touch, his strong, calloused palm warm against her skin.

"This guy sounds dangerous, Iz. Just promise me you'll be careful."

Why does he have to be so damn sweet?

"Seems like you're the one who needs to be careful, Detective." Izzy ignored the fluttering in her stomach and kept her expression playful. "Better watch yourself, or I might begin to think you actually care."

A flash of pain darkened his gaze a fraction of a second before he rumbled, "Casual doesn't mean heartless, sweetheart." Grady's throat worked with a swallow. "And for the record, I do care."

So do I. That's what makes this next part so damn hard.

Dropping her hand, Izzy put some space back between them. Despite the struggle within, she ignored the voice screaming in her head that this was wrong and did what she had to do.

For Grady's sake.

"I wanted to talk to you about that, actually." Licking her dry lips nervously, she prayed he couldn't see the internal struggle warring inside her that very moment. "I think it's time for us both to move on."

"Move on?" Those mesmerizing eyes of his widened, his dark brows arching high. "So that's it? You're ending things, just like that?"

Izzy crossed her arms in front of her, the urge to reach out to him and tell him she'd changed her mind tempting as hell. "It's nothing personal, Grady. You know I like you. And...I care about you, too. It's just that everything's been crazier than normal lately at work. For the both of us." She added that last part belatedly. "Even you have to agree we've barely been able to find the time for each other these last two months. And with your court case coming up and the stack of consults currently piled high on my desk, it's not likely to get better anytime soon. Besides we both agreed this wouldn't be anything more than what it's been. And it's not like either of us expected our...whatever this thing between us has been...to go the distance. Right?"

God, she hated how callous she'd sounded. As if the time spent with Grady had meant nothing to her. In reality, it had meant more than he'd ever know.

And more than I'll ever admit.

The muscular man ran a hand over his beard and chuckled. "Nah, you're right. We both agreed there'd be no strings or expectations. I guess I'm just a little surprised you're ready to be done, given that you spent last night in my bed. What was that? One last round in the sack for old time's sake?"

"What? No!" Izzy frowned. "I hadn't planned on...this... until this morning. And before you say it, this has nothing to do with last night or any other night we've spent together. I know right now you probably don't believe me, but I really do like you, Grady. More than I've liked anyone in a very, very long time. But like I said when we first started, I don't do relationships. And I thought..." *Don't cry, Iz. Whatever you do, you* cannot *cry!* "I thought we were alike in that way."

"You're right." He shoved his hands into his pockets. "I did say that, and now I'm being a dick. I apologize."

"You're not being a dick. And I'm the one who should apologize. If things were different...if *I* was different..." She blew out a breath. "There isn't anyone I'd rather do serious with than you. But I just can't. I'm sorry."

Grady's expression softened, his taut thighs carrying him closer. Cupping her cheek with one of his talented hands, he looked her straight in the eyes and softly told her, "You ever change your mind about wanting more, I'd be open to discussing it."

Well, hell. "Thank you, but I'm afraid that ship has sailed for me." Rising onto her tiptoes, Izzy pressed a soft, sweet kiss to his lips. "See you around, big guy. Stay safe out there."

"You, too."

With that, Izzy stepped out of his reach, got into her car, and drove away. And as she drove down the steady decline toward the parking garage entrance, she allowed herself one final glance in the rearview before finally letting the tears fall.

2

Two days later...

"That's it."

"Wha—" Grady's question was cut short by the need to brace himself as his partner yanked the steering wheel sharply to the right. Their department-issued car swerved toward the shoulder of the road. With his upper arm pressed against the passenger window, Grady's head and torso jerked forward with the vehicle's sudden stop. "What the hell's the matter with you?"

Declan King, Grady's partner in Denver P.D.'s elite Major Crimes Unit, shoved the gearshift into park and turned to face him. "Funny. I was about to ask you the same thing."

"Me?" His brows shot up. "I was just sitting here!"

"Exactly." Declan's dark eyes studied him closely.

Thoroughly confused now, Grady tilted his head and narrowed his eyes. "You just went all Dukes of Hazard on me because I'm...sitting?"

"I pulled over because you've barely said two words since we got in the car. In fact, you've been unusually quiet the last couple of days, which is not like you at all. Now, I've tried to give you your space and respect your privacy, but now I'm starting to worry. So start talking."

Shit. He hadn't realized he'd been acting differently around Dec or the others. In fact, Grady had *thought* he'd been doing a bang-up job at hiding his disappointment over Izzy ending things between them.

Apparently you thought wrong.

"I'm fine," Grady lied. "No need to worry."

"Bullshit," the experienced detective called his bluff. "We've been partners for almost a year, Grady. Surely in that time, you've learned I'm not a stupid man."

"Never said you were."

"Then quit acting like I am, and talk to me."

Don't do it. Don't do it...

"I'm good, man," he lied a second time. "Really. I just haven't felt the best lately, so I haven't slept all that great, either."

Not exactly another lie. More like a vague deception. He truly *didn't* feel the best, and he hadn't been sleeping worth a shit.

But it had nothing to do with his health, as he hoped Declan would assume.

"Oh." His partner blinked. "Sorry. Could be that stomach bug that's going around. Heard that's been knocking quite a few people on their asses lately."

"Maybe." Grady shrugged. "Who knows?"

He did. *He* knew what ailed him, and it sure as hell wasn't a stomach virus.

I miss her. I know I'm not supposed to, but I do.

Grady glanced at his phone, wishing like hell she'd call.

It had been two full days since Izzy cut things off between them. Two days of trying not to think about the mouthwatering woman.

And it was driving him crazy.

"Just make sure you don't breathe on me." Declan chuckled as he pulled the car back onto the road and resumed driving. "Skye will kill me if I get sick before the wedding."

Despite his sour mood, Grady felt his lips lifting at the corners. "You ready?"

"To marry Skye?" The other man's face lit up with the same goofy grin he'd been wearing for months. "I can't fucking wait. You're still going, right?"

"Wouldn't miss it."

"Better not."

"Don't worry, Dec. I'll be there." He added a teasing, "Besides, those reservations are non-refundable. Can't just let that money slip away."

His partner smirked. "Glad to see you have your priorities in line."

With a chuckle, Grady slapped Declan's arm. "Ah, come on, brother. You know I'm just playin'. I can't wait to see you and Skye tie the knot." He swallowed. "I'm happy for you, Dec. Still not sure how you landed such a great catch, but...."

"You *trying* to get your ass uninvited?"

"Never gonna happen. That pretty fiancée of yours loves me too much."

Mouth open, Declan was clearly preparing to let loose a witty comeback when his phone began to ring. Keeping one hand on the wheel, he pulled the device from his jacket pocket and checked the screen.

"It's Riedell." He slid his thumb across the screen and put the phone on speaker. "Hey, Sarge. Got you on speaker. Thorne and I are almost to Torres' apartment. Everything good with the warrant?"

Alvaro Torres was a person of interest in their unit's latest unsolved homicide investigation. One of three that had recently dropped into their laps. All three men were of Hispanic descent. All of various ages. But there were two distinct connections linking the three dead men to each other.

One was they all had each been definitively tied to the Los Reyes. Spanish for *The Kings*, the criminal faction was the largest Mexican gang currently active in Denver.

The other connection shared by each of their vics was cause of death. All three men had been executed by way of a single gunshot to the back of the head. Abrasions found during autopsy suggested the ill-fated gang members had been on their knees at the time of their deaths.

And Alvaro Torres was spotted by an eyewitness—and CCTV cams—running hella fast a block away from their latest crime scene.

"That's why I'm calling," Sergeant Riedell's raspy voice came back through the phone's speakers. "Eden and Archer are headed your way with the papers."

"You want us to wait?" Grady posed the question to their boss.

"No need. Judge Mitchell signed the warrant, and it should be there in ten. But if you get there and smell something off, wait for backup."

"Copy that, Sarge. I'll let you know when we're headed back to the district."

"Watch your backs." The stoic man ended the call.

Declan slid the phone back into his jacket pocket. "One less thing to worry about."

Grady nodded in agreement. "Good to know the judge has our backs with this one."

"Mitchell's as solid as they come." The other man slowed the car to prepare a right-hand turn. "She has a passion for justice, and it shows. More importantly, Judge Mitchell never lets politics or money sway her decisions in the courtroom."

"Sounds like my kind of woman."

The comment was meant to be flippant, but his partner used it as an open invitation to move their topic of conversation to Grady's personal life.

"Funny. I thought tall, dark, and sexy psychiatrists were more your type."

"And *I* thought I told *you* a dozen times already, there's nothing between Izzy and me."

"Oh, you did." A left turn. "I just don't believe you."

"You a human lie detector now?"

"No, I'm your partner. And I think I've gotten to know you pretty well these last ten, almost eleven months. Come on, man. You can trust me. I promise I won't say anything to anyone."

"Not even Skye?"

Declan waited to park the car next to the curb before answering. Putting it into park, he swung his gaze to Grady's and raised two fingers. "Whatever you say will stay between us, Scout's honor."

It was a tempting offer, but no. Grady didn't tell him about Izzy because there wasn't anything *to* tell. Not anymore.

There isn't anyone I'd rather do serious with than you. But I just can't. I'm sorry.

He must have replayed those words in his head a million times since she'd uttered them. There was so much pain hiding behind those gorgeous eyes of hers, and Grady found himself wanting nothing more than to erase it. To replace it with light filled with joy and laughter and happiness.

And to find the bastard responsible for creating that pain in the first place.

In the months he and Izzy had been seeing each other, they'd kept the depth of their conversations to a minimum. Sure, they'd talked about all the typical get-to-know-you things.

How they got started in their respective fields. Where they grew up. What their childhoods were like.

He'd shared with her a few short stories about the trouble he and his younger brother had gotten into when they were kids. Only Izzy had never given him specifics on what things were like for her as a child.

And every time Grady had pushed for more, she was always quick to change the subject. Usually distracting him with her talented mouth.

It wasn't like he couldn't find the answers he craved. A quick look into her background would do the trick. But every time he'd started to, Grady talked himself out of it.

Sleeping together or not, Izzy's private life was just that. Private. And her past was her own story to tell.

As tempting as it was, he'd never violate her privacy by running her like a common criminal. For several reasons. Mainly it was because he'd hoped to hear it straight from her.

I wanted her to trust me.

Unfortunately for him, it didn't really matter what he wanted. And it wasn't like he even had the right to be upset.

Like she'd reminded him, keeping things casual between them was originally his idea.

Brilliant, Thorne. Fucking brilliant.

"Sorry to burst your bubble, Dec, but what I said is true." He unbuckled his seatbelt and opened the passenger door. "There's nothing between Izzy and me. Now can we please focus on why we're here?"

Rather than waiting for a response, Grady stepped out onto the cracked and broken curb. On reflex, he slid the dark sunglasses from the top of his smooth head as he shut the door behind him.

"Fine." Declan shut the driver's door and walked around the front bumper. "I'll drop it."

About damn time. "Thank you."

Minutes later, the two men were standing in the dimly lit hallway just outside their suspect's door. Weathered and worn, its once vibrant color had been reduced to a mere memory under the weight of time. Its peeling paint bore witness to the squalor and desperation of the neighborhood they found themselves in.

Grady raised his fist and pounded against the paint-chipped surface, the rising pulse and slight rush of adrenaline coursing through him all too familiar. His voice authoritative as he announced their presence to those who might be inside.

"Denver Police Department! Open up!"

Silence greeted his demand, stretching the tension hanging thick in the musty air. But just as doubt of Torres' presence began creeping into Grady's mind, a crashing sound shattered the stillness.

Instinctively, Grady and Declan exchanged a knowing look, their hands tightening around the grips of their drawn weapons. Though they'd been partners less than a full year, the two seasoned detectives already shared an unspoken connection honed by months of working side by side.

Without hesitation, Grady lifted his booted foot and kicked in the door. The frame shattered as it swung open with a bang.

They stormed into the apartment, eyes scanning the scene with hawk-like intensity. But their suspect was one step ahead, already climbing out of a window and onto the fire escape.

"Go!" Declan's urgent voice cut through the chaos. "I'll catch up!" He dashed toward the window, his trained eyes locked on their fleeing perp.

Trusting his partner to handle the pursuit, Grady nodded and swiftly turned on his heels. He sprinted down the apartment's narrow, creaking staircase. Each step echoing with his determination as he made his swift descent.

The world blurred around him as he burst through the building's exit, his boots pounding on the pavement as he ran. Grady pushed himself to his limits, the wind whipping against his face as he raced down the block and plunged into the alley.

As he rounded the corner, his eyes caught a glimpse of the suspect who was mere steps away from freedom. There was no time for doubts or second guesses.

Grady moved on instinct, his muscles coiling with lethal precision. Like a force of nature, he launched himself forward with his non-weapon arm stretched horizontally to his side. In an effort to stop Torres, Grady used his powerful forearm to strike the fleeing man in the chest.

The blow sent both men spinning, the world around them swirling momentarily as the criminal's momentum faltered. With a guttural grunt, Torres crashed to the ground.

"What did I do?" The suspect's voice sounded strained as his arms were pulled behind his back. "Man, I didn't do nothin'!"

"No?" Grady secured the final cuff, his breath labored as he yanked a pistol from Torres' back waistband. "Then why'd you run?"

"You're cops." Torres continued with his games. "It's in my blood to run when the pigs come knockin'."

A winded Declan joined them, his dark brows arching high. With a grin lifting one corner of his lips, he took the offered weapon before helping Grady pull their suspect to his feet.

"Pigs?" Dec blew out a huffed breath. "Now that's just hurtful, Alvie."

"How do you know my name?"

"Alvarez Hugo Torres," Grady recited their perp's full name and then his Miranda Rights. "You have the right to remain silent..."

Seconds later, the visibly agitated criminal tried jerking himself free. "Don't know what you think you have on me, but I don't know nothin' about nothin'."

"Your arrest warrant disagrees." Movement to Grady's left caught his attention. "Speak of the devil."

Detectives Jacobs and Eden had just exited their vehicle and were making their way to the party.

Standing right at six-feet, thirty-two-year-old Blake Jacobs had joined Major Crimes a year before Grady made the move from Chicago to Denver. The man had short brown hair, dark eyes, and a face women fell all over themselves to gawk at.

Blake's counterpart, however, was about as opposite

from Jacobs as she could get. But Kimberly Eden was every bit as capable as any man on their team.

Though you wouldn't think it at first glance, the five-foot-nothing former beauty queen was a trained sniper. The pretty blonde was also one of the sharpest, most dogged detectives Grady had ever had the pleasure of working with.

Just like the rest of his new unit.

"Damn." Blake offered them a cocky grin. "Looks like we missed all the fun."

"Fun. Sure." Grady began leading Torres toward his and Declan's car. "That's what we'll call it."

Torres kept on with his empty vows and bullshit innocent act. The grip Grady had on the other man's arm tightened, his voice carrying the weight of authority as he gave their suspect instructions.

"Stand here and don't move."

In minutes, the entire block was filled with lights of blue and red. The ride back to the station felt miles longer than it actually was, thanks to Torres' non-stop yapping. But by the time Grady and Dec had him cuffed to a table in one of their unit's six interrogation rooms, the arrogant gang member's attitude quickly changed.

"Recognize these?" Grady slapped three eight-by-tens on the table in front of Torres.

Without so much as a sideways glance, their suspect shook his head with a quipped, "Nope."

"Look at the pictures, Alvarez." Declan's order was stern.

The young thug kept his stare forward.

Grady smiled. Pulling out a chair, he sat down in front of Torres and began gathering up the first two pictures. "That's okay, Alvie. These two aren't that important, anyway. Because we've already got you on this one…" He picked up the third picture and held it directly in front of the other man's face.

Though it was slight, Grady noticed a small twitch of Torres' right eye.

There it is.

"That's right, Alvie. We can place you at the scene of the crime the night poor Juan Gomez was shot."

"You've got the wrong guy."

"Actually, we've got the exact *right* guy." Declan picked up a remote and activated the wall-mounted flatscreen in the corner of the small room.

The three watched the CCTV footage showcasing none other than Alvarez Torres.

"See that guy running there?" Grady turned his serious gaze back to the young convict. "That's you. And according to the timestamp on this video, it matches the medical examiner's estimated time of death for Gomez."

"There's an eyewitness, too," Declan chimed back in. "That's two positive ID's making you the last person to see Gomez alive. And I'm willing to bet the ballistics from the gun we took off you matches the bullet the ME pulled out of Gomez's brain. Oh, and just so you have all the facts, evidence suggests Gomez was forced to his knees before he was killed. You know what that's called, Alvie?"

Both detectives waited, but the twenty-something asshat pursed his lips and remained silent.

"First degree murder," Grady announced sternly. "That's life in Colorado."

A flash of real emotion filled Torres' eyes for the first time since getting clotheslined in that alley. It was the turning point they needed.

Declan took the seat beside Grady, glancing down at the manila folder in his hands. "Says here you're twenty-two.

That's damn near half the average inmate age. Now given that the average man lives to be seventy-four, and that's living on the outside with comfortable shelter, healthy food options, regular exercise, and doctor visits."

"My partner makes a good point, Alvie." Grady spoke up again. "That means your home for the next fifty-two years will be an eight-by-eight concrete cell. And that's assuming you don't fall victim to a rival gang member or someone looking for revenge."

"Or some guy who's bored on a Tuesday afternoon," his partner snorted.

"That's right." Grady nodded, his appreciative look not going unnoticed. "Some of those guys will cut you just to cut you."

"Or worse."

"What's worse than being shivved to death?" Torres shot Declan an incredulous look. When Grady and Dec both shot him a knowing shrug, the kid's face fell.

Grady smiled. "I think he might finally be getting it, Detective King."

"I believe you're right, Detective Thorne. But we should probably make sure, just in case."

"What my partner is so politely trying to say is the whole cliché about going to prison and becoming some big dude's bitch…" He shrugged. "All I can say is the cliché exists for a reason."

"That's a good point." Declan nodded. "I've seen countless guys get sent to the infirmary with internal damage as a result. But I'm sure you'll be fine."

Grady followed his partner's lead. "The worst part will probably be not having any privacy. Depending on where they send you, you'll probably have a cellmate. Can't sleep alone, can't eat alone—"

"Can't go to the bathroom alone," Dec continued. "Hope you're not shy because once you're there, you'll be showering and shitting with a slew of your closest friends right there by your side."

The longer they talked, the more the color drained from Torres' face.

"I want a deal."

The detectives shared a look before Declan reached down and picked up the final picture. "Sorry." He stood. "The time for deals is over."

When Grady rose to his feet and began following his partner toward the room's secured door, Torres practically ripped his hands off trying to stand and chase after them.

"Wait!" The sound of metal clanged, the cuff's edges striking against the two rings held in place on the table. The quad of unbendable steel bolts halted his movements, jerking the idiot back down to his seat. "I've got a name!"

Both men halted their steps. With his hand hovering over the door's metal handle, Declan slid his focus back to Torres. "Who?"

"Nah, man." Torres shook his head. "First, we make the deal, and then I tell you. Otherwise, I'm as good as dead."

"You're going to rot behind bars if you don't tell us." Declan's stone-cold gaze never wavered. "And that's *if* you don't catch a knife to the gut before then."

When the kid hesitated, Grady walked back over to the table. "I'd listen to my partner, Alvie. You're gonna do time. There's no way around that. But we can work with the DA on the location of your facility and the duration of your stay...*if* the intel you give us pans out."

"Oh, it'll pan out. No doubt."

"This is your one chance, Alvarez." Declan came to

Grady's side. "Give us a name right now, or there's no deal. We'll check out your story. If it all adds up, we'll talk deal."

Torres opened his mouth and closed it. He repeated the fish-out-of-water move three separate times before he finally, *finally* started talking.

"I give you a name, you'll make sure I go someplace safe?"

"If by safe, you mean a prison with no known Los Reyes crew—"

"Or rival gangs," Torres cut through Dec's words.

His fear clearly stemmed not only from whoever put him up to killing Juan Gomez, but also those he and his fellow Reyes had crossed.

Play stupid games...

"That might be a bit trickier," Declan responded. "But I promise we'll do everything we can to place you somewhere safe."

It wasn't an empty promise. Their unit had a close working relationship with the DA's office, and Riedell trusted the team's judgement enough to back them up.

"You swear on my mama's grave."

"You have our word." Grady locked eyes with the young man. And then...

"Dante Valdez."

Beside him, Declan's spine visibly stiffened. "Dante Valdez, the *businessman*?"

"Why do I know that name?" Grady turned to his partner, but it was Torres who answered.

"Ever heard of La Cocina? Valdez owns it."

"I've heard of it," he confirmed. "It's that high-end Mexican restaurant across from The Capital Grille." Another really nice eating establishment in town.

"That's the one." Torres nodded. "Valdez owns it and several other properties in the city."

"He's also well-connected and well-respected."

"Don't you mean feared?" Their prisoner slid his knowing gaze to Dec's.

"What do you mean by that?"

Settling back in the weighted metal chair—its legs designed to keep it on the floor in case an arrestee happened to get loose from their cuffs—Torres shrugged. "Just what I said. On the outside, Valdez comes off like gold. But you dig a little deeper, you'll find all sorts of folks hiding in the pockets of those designer suits of his. Including every member of Los Reyes. And rumor has it, some of the folks Valdez keeps close wear blue. Just like you two."

The only blue Grady and Dec were currently wearing was the denim of their jeans, but both detectives understood the guy's meaning. Dante Valdez had not only ordered Torres to execute a Los Reyes gang member, but he'd also had people within the DPD on his payroll. Supposedly.

"You got names for these men and women in blue?" Grady watched and waited, but the response he got wasn't what he'd hoped for.

"You think they'd tell a guy like me something that big?" Sarcastic laughter echoed off the concrete walls. "Trust me, I'm not that important. Hell, I'm one of a handful of enforcers Valdez has working for him. My guess is those other two stiffs you guys found belong to one of them."

Declan drew in a deep breath and let it out slowly. "So let me get this straight. You were given a direct order from Dante Valdez to kill Juan Gomez, and you just...did it. Did you even bother to ask your boss *why* he wanted one of your brothers dead?"

"Man, I get paid to do as I'm told not ask questions."

"And Gomez didn't say anything to you before you pulled the trigger?"

Another chuckle. "That little bitch said all kinds of things. He begged me to let him go. Made promises I knew the entitled thief would never keep. Poor bastard even cried for his mama at the end."

Jesus. "Back up," Grady instructed. "You called Gomez a lying thief. What did he steal?"

"I don't know for sure. No firsthand knowledge or anything like that. But rumor among the brothers is Gomez was skimming from the boss."

"Money?"

"Money, drugs…women. Like I said, Gomez was entitled. Thought he was owed for all his hard work. Never mind the stacks of cash Valdez throws our way."

"That's all really good information, Alvarez," Declan commended. "What would you think about going back in and getting more?"

"You want me to be y'all's snitch?" Torres' voice rose two octaves. "Ah, hell no. I'd rather take my chances in prison."

Not one to give up easily, Declan kept on. "You'd wear a wire. Our tech guys are really good at what they do. They have some so small, they're nearly impossible to detect."

"We'd be able to see and hear everything you do," Grady piggybacked off his partner's comments. "We'd be right outside the whole time."

But Torres clearly wanted no part in it.

"Forget it." He shook his head with vigor. "Nah, that wasn't the deal. I gave you a name. A *big* one. You want anything else, you'll have to find another snitch."

"What if we could get the DA to give you a reduced sentence? He might agree to cut your time short."

"I'm good." Torres' definitive answer surprised both

detectives. "I'd rather take my chances on the inside than with Valdez. He finds out I snitched, a bullet to the head will be a blessing compared to what he'll do."

"We can protect you," Grady promised. "Might even be a chance for you to go into Witness Pro—"

"Witness Protection? Shit, man." The cuffed man smirked. "Those dudes get found and popped all the time, from what I hear."

"That's not true."

"No? Why? 'Cause you, the *cop*, says so?" Torres leaned in closer, his forearms and elbows fully rested on the table in front of him. Keeping full eye contact, he lowered his voice to a calm, unwavering tone. "You want more on Dante Valdez, go do your jobs and find it. I'm done."

Sitting back in his chair, the murdering S.O.B. made a show of looking away. A physical sign that he was, in fact, finished talking. A shared glance between partners was all that was needed for Grady and Declan to agree.

If they wanted more evidence on Dante Valdez, they were going to have to find it some other way.

As he and Dec left the interrogation room, Grady's thoughts momentarily turned to Izzy. Not long ago, he and the sexy psychiatrist had shared a brief but passionate moment in that exact same room.

It happened right after she'd nearly given him a heart attack by putting herself smack dab in the middle of a hostage situation.

Though their physical relationship had been just that—physical and without strings—in those final moments leading up to the hostage taker's apprehension, Grady had felt a level of fear unlike any he'd ever known.

Which was saying something, given that he started his career as a cop in Chicago.

That day changed everything for him. He started contemplating his life choices and goals. Started really looking at where he wanted to be in five, ten, twenty years.

While it wasn't intentional, every future Grady envisioned for himself included Izzy.

He'd kept those thoughts close to the vest, of course. Never once talking about it with Declan or any other member of his unit.

He sure as hell hadn't brought it up with Izzy. She'd made herself crystal clear in the beginning that serious wasn't an option.

So Grady kept his burgeoning feelings for the sexy brunette locked down to avoid scaring her off. Which, as it turns out, was a non-issue since she'd already broken things off.

A move that still gnawed at his gut. Not because he couldn't imagine any woman not wanting to be with him. Grady might see a decent-looking guy staring back at him from the mirror, but he was far from perfect. And he was *not* one of those guys who believed himself to be irresistible to the female population.

But Izzy was different. When she walked into a room, everything else around him just seemed to disappear.

Only Grady continually ignored the signs that this woman was different from the rest. That she was special. By the time he realized he might actually want to move out of the casual lovers' stage and into something real, it was too late.

I missed my chance.

The big bad detective, who took on gunfire without flinching and took down criminals littering his city's streets, had missed the opportunity to finally have something real—

something meaningful—with an amazing, intelligent woman.

But if she ever changes her mind...

Grady had no way of knowing if that would ever happen. But he'd sure as hell already made up his. If he got the chance again...if Izzy gave him the green light to start things back up again in the future, he was going to roll the dice and see where they landed. After all...

What do I have to lose?

3

Izzy's heels clicked across the hardwood floor as she walked toward Sergeant Riedell's office. The man in charge of Denver's Major Crimes Unit—and Grady's boss—had reached out earlier, asking if she would meet with him at her earliest convenience.

When he'd first contacted her, Izzy was about to start a psych assessment for a juvenile offender being treated at a hospital across town. She hated making Riedell wait, especially given the kinds of cases Grady's team worked, but deep down, she'd welcomed the unavoidable delay.

It had been two full days since that painfully awkward conversation with Grady in the parking garage. Since then, she hadn't seen or heard from him and was unsure of how she'd react if she did.

Normally when Izzy ended things with a lover, a full-stop closure was exactly what she wanted. But with Grady...

I miss him.

She didn't usually miss anyone other than her parents and brother. But there was just something about the sexy detective that stirred up all sorts of unwanted feelings.

Not that it mattered.

Sure he'd appeared disappointed by her decision to break things off. At first. But it hadn't taken long for him to become agreeable, allowing the moment to pass cordially.

The unexpected disappointment Izzy had felt in that moment was a crushing blow she hadn't seen coming. She wasn't supposed to want more or look for him everywhere she went. She wasn't supposed to lie awake at night, replaying their most sensual moments together in her head.

And she absolutely was *not* supposed to care.

So when she arrived at Grady's place of work, Izzy couldn't help but feel relieved to find him nowhere in sight. Luckily—from what she'd overheard while walking through the bullpen—he and his partner were running down a possible lead across town.

Avoidance much?

Ignoring the tugging at her heart, Izzy raised a fist and knocked on Sergeant Riedell's door. Through the frosted window, she could see the formidable man waving for her She turned the knob and stepped inside.

Her steps faltered when she realized they weren't alone.

"SAC Hunt." She greeted the special agent in charge of Denver's lead FBI team with a firm handshake and a smile. "It's an honor to meet you. I've heard nothing but good things about you and your team."

Though Izzy hadn't personally worked with them, it was common knowledge around the local law enforcement family that Hunt's unit was the best in the Bureau.

"Likewise, Dr. Garcia." Hunt returned the handshake.

Turning to her left, Izzy held out her hand to a stunning woman she'd never seen before. "Dr. Isobel Garcia. I'm the department's forensic psychiatrist."

"Assistant District Attorney Camille Umbridge." The

thirty-something redhead smiled as she took Izzy's hand in hers. "It's a pleasure, Dr. Garcia. And please, call me Cam."

"Izzy."

The two women shared a nod before Izzy returned her focus to the man who'd summoned her here. "I apologize for making you all wait."

"I just appreciate you working us into your schedule." Riedell pulled his chair out so he could sit. "Please."

He motioned toward one of two empty chairs facing him. When Izzy sat in the one closest to where she stood, Cam followed her lead and took the remaining seat.

Turning his voice serious, the man in charge of the room rested his forearms on the smooth surface in front of him, linking his fingers together. "We've all got jobs to do, so I'll get straight to the point." His wise eyes lasered in on hers. "Dr. Garcia, we have a delicate situation on our hands, and we believe you can help us."

She arched a brow, her curiosity piqued. "Of course, Sergeant. How can I assist?"

SAC Hunt approached from Izzy's right. Placing a manila folder on the desk directly in front of her, he flipped it open for her to see.

Izzy leaned forward to get a closer look at what appeared to be a surveillance photo paper-clipped to a small stack of papers and notes. She studied the printed image closely, her breath catching in her throat as she realized what—or more accurately, *who*—she was looking at.

"Olly."

She hadn't uttered her estranged brother's name aloud in over two years. Hadn't seen him or spoken to him since he called one morning to tell her he was leaving town...again.

Olly—short for Oliver—did that. He'd pop into Denver,

stay for a while, and either get into trouble and get arrested or split before that could happen.

Either way, Izzy lived every day with the knowledge that *she* was the reason his life was so screwed up. And it killed her.

She studied the picture again. Her earliest memories of Olly were of him as a young boy. Short brown hair, big round eyes. Dimples and the biggest, sweetest smile. The most contagious laugh...

Just like Mom's.

But that was before.

Before a drunk driver shattered their perfect, all-American world by stealing two of the most amazing, loving parents who'd ever existed. Before Izzy and her older brother were thrown into a system that was so overcrowded and understaffed, it was all too easy for kids like them to fall through the cracks.

For reasons she still didn't fully understand, Izzy somehow made it through to the other side. Not totally unscathed—she still carried scars from that time in her life. But she'd survived.

By the grace of God, she'd survived and had come out the other side with a fierce need to understand the human psyche. To make sense of what drove humans to make this choice versus that, to grow up to be inherently good while others...

So many others don't.

Due to Izzy's craving for answers, she'd worked her ass off and put herself through school hoping to help others.

Olly, however...

If a kid gets knocked down by life too often, he'll eventually start punching back.

Her brother's face came back into focus. Not the same

one she remembered as a child, or even from the last time she saw him. This Olly seemed to have aged exponentially since then.

He was still handsome, of course. Her brother had always been a looker, as her mom had called him. But this version of her brother was a man with too much life behind him. Too much pain.

His broad shoulders appeared almost hunched, as if they carried the weight of the world, and his weathered skin marked by dark shadows. New sprigs of silver already starting to sprout at his temples.

But it was the look of defeat in her brother's eyes that left unshed tears in Izzy's. As if he'd given up on life just as life had given up on him.

Preventing an embarrassing show of emotions in front of her colleagues, she blinked away the moisture and studied the entire picture, not just Olly.

In it, he was carrying a box toward the opened back of a cargo van, his impressive biceps stretching the short sleeves of his T. Behind him was a loading dock connected to a building made of tan bricks with light gray mortar, and there was an open side door to the far right.

That was it. There was no illegal activity going on that she could see. Nothing nefarious or glaringly obvious.

In fact, the only thing Izzy *was* clear on was that, at the time the picture was taken, her brother had no idea he was being watched. Let alone photographed.

Izzy pulled it free from the paperclip holding it in place. When she did, all the papers in the file shifted, revealing a handful of additional loose photos fanning out behind them.

Gathering them up, she began to go through them. One by one, she studied several more pictures of Olly. His clothing was different in each of them, the lighting and time of day changing with each flip of the stack.

The authorities—presumably the FBI, since SAC Hunt was here—had obviously been watching her brother over what appeared to be a course of several days. Possibly weeks or even months.

What the hell?

"Dr. Garcia—"

"Izzy," she muttered the correction to SAC Hunt while once again staring intently at the glossy five-by-sevens still in her hands.

Her heart ached knowing Olly was back in Denver and he hadn't bothered to call or come by. Or even shoot her a text.

You ruined his life. Can you blame him?

"Izzy, have you ever heard of a man named Dante Valdez?"

"No." She shook her head, her eyes refusing to leave the frozen image of her only living relative. "Should I have?"

"Dante Valdez is a well-known businessman here in town," Sgt. Riedell explained. "He owns La Cocina—"

"The restaurant?" Izzy cut him off as she met the man's stare. "I've eaten there several times. It's quite good."

"It's a popular place." Riedell nodded. "And Valdez is a smart man. Especially when it comes to business and money."

"He owns several rental properties in town, does a lot of charity work, rubs elbows with Denver's rich and powerful..." Cam shot her a look and a muttered, "You get the idea."

"I still don't understand what this has to do with Olly."

"For months now, the Feds have suspected Valdez of running a major trafficking business right here in Denver,"

Hunt explained, his expression intense. "We're talking drugs, weapons...sex. He has known ties to a local Mexican gang who go by the name Los Reyes."

"The Kings." Izzy translated the Spanish name easily before looking up to meet Hunt's serious gaze.

"You speak Spanish." The comment came from an impressed Cam.

Izzy nodded silently, her eyes still on the stoic FBI leader. "So this Valdez guy is near the top of Denver's social food chain." They'd made that point clear. "I still don't understand what this has to do with Olly."

Or me.

"My team's had two fresh bodies drop in our laps in the last six weeks." Grady's boss laid out two new pictures, the lifeless faces of two young men lying dead on what she assumed was an autopsy table. And then, "Number three was discovered today." He placed a third picture out for her to see. "All three men were executed with a single bullet to the back of their heads. And all three men have known ties to the Los Reyes."

Another picture. Another life. All three cut down decades too short.

Izzy closed her eyes and turned her head, despite knowing it was too late. The faces of the dead had already solidified themselves in her memory.

Just like so many others.

"See that warehouse there?" Riedell reached across the desk to point at the section of building seen in the photo's background. "It's owned by Valdez. According to our intel, your brother has worked there for the past two months."

"You said Dante Valdez owned one of the hottest restaurants in town, as well as several other properties?" Her question was posed to the room.

SAC Hunt answered with a deep and gruff, "So?"

Placing the photos back onto the still-open file folder, Izzy settled back into her chair. "So it stands to reason he employs several legitimate men and women to run the day-to-day operation of those businesses. Wouldn't you say?"

Because she was starting to understand at least part of why she was here.

They think Olly's involved in a human trafficking ring.

"You sure that fancy degree of yours didn't come from a law school?" Cam quipped.

The attractive woman's tone was lighthearted, the curved smile lifting her ruby lips holding no ill-will or sarcastic feel. But Izzy wasn't in the mood to joke. Not about this.

"I'm just pointing out that a few photos of my brother at work doesn't mean his association with Valdez is anything less than the up-and-up."

"You're absolutely right," SAC Hunt agreed. "Which is why your brother is still walking around a free man."

"That and the fact that you clearly have no solid, undeniable proof of Valdez's criminal activity," Izzy shot back. "Otherwise he'd already be in prison."

"And when it comes to Valdez, the case against him has to be airtight." Cam rested a gentle hand on Izzy's forearm. "That's where you come in. Or more accurately, that's where *Olly* comes in."

"Olly?" She frowned. "How can my brother help?"

"The FBI has been watching Valdez closely over the last few months," Hunt finally got to the point. "We have eyes on him, each of his businesses...and every employee we believe might possibly be involved in the off-the-books stuff."

"It's why you're here." Sgt. Riedell stared back at her. "Our most recent homicide victim is a twenty-one-year-old kid named Juan Gomez. He was forced to his knees and shot in the back of the head by another young man by the name of Alvarez Torres, a Los Reyes gang member we currently have in custody."

"According to Mr. Torres, it was Dante Valdez who ordered the hit."

Cam said this as if it explained everything, when, in reality, it left Izzy feeling even more confused.

"That's good, right?" She turned to the other woman with an expectant look. "This Torres guy...the one you're holding for Gomez's murder...he can testify to the fact and put Valdez away for good."

I don't understand what the problem is.

"That's the problem," Cam answered as if she could read Izzy's mind. "The kid did confess to the killing, and he told Detectives King and Thorne that Valdez was behind it. But when they brought up the idea of getting Valdez on tape admitting he was the one who ordered Juan Gomez's execution, he refused."

"And as much as we'd love to"—Riedell continued where the pretty ADA left off—"we can't force the kid to do or say more than he already has."

Izzy sat up a little straighter, the gnawing in her gut growing stronger with each unclear second that passed. "You just said Torres has already confessed to the murder, and he's handed you Valdez on a silver platter."

"Not exactly." Hunt shook his head. "As far as Valdez's involvement in Gomez's execution, it's Torres' word against his."

"Unfortunately, it's going to take a lot more than a murdering gang member's testimony to put a man like Valdez away."

From the look in Cam's sparkling blue eyes, Izzy could

easily see the other woman's frustration with the many flaws of their current justice system.

Trust me, I know the feeling.

Addressing the entire room, Izzy cleared her throat and ran through a brief recap to make sure she was caught up to speed.

"Okay, so let me see if I have everything straight. You have three dead Los Reyes gang members, one definitively shot by one of their own, and that man is claiming Dante Valdez ordered the killing." Which, in her non-lawyer, non-cop mind seemed like a slam-dunk. "But you're saying you need more evidence against Valdez in order to solidify a conviction, and since Olly works for Valdez, you want him to…do what exactly?"

"We need your brother to wear a camera and a wire," SAC Hunt announced bluntly. "He gets Valdez on tape admitting he was behind the hit, we've got him."

That gnawing morphed into full-blown nausea. "You want Olly to go undercover for you? That's…" She glanced around the small office space praying she'd heard wrong. "My brother isn't a cop."

Not by a long shot.

"No, he's a convict who did time for breaking and entering and assault."

Izzy huffed out a soft, sarcastic chuckle. "I see you don't pull any punches, do you Agent Hunt?"

His answer was as unapologetic as his previous statement.

"Pulling punches delays results, Dr. Garcia. And when we're dealing with a man like Dante Valdez, every second counts."

"Look, Izzy." Cam spoke up again. "We all understand how big of an ask this is for your brother. The stakes are high, and the risks are very real. But Valdez needs to be stopped, and unfortunately the bastard always seems to be one step ahead of the DPD and the FBI. The simple fact is, we need more evidence, and the only way we're going to get it is from the inside."

"So send in an undercover cop." Izzy swung her gaze to Sgt. Riedell's. "Surely someone on your team has experience with this sort of thing."

Just not Grady. Please don't send him into the lion's den.

Sure, Grady was well-trained and knew what he was doing when it came to his job. From what she'd seen during the past several months, the sexy detective was more than capable of handling himself.

But still...

Izzy didn't want *anyone* she cared about anywhere near a man like Dante Valdez. And she did care about Grady. More than she ever intended.

"My team's worked security detail on a few local political fundraisers in the past," Grady's boss explained why her idea wouldn't work. "Valdez has been in attendance at some of those, which means he might recognize one of them."

"Okay, well...the department's a big one." She kept trying. "Put someone else in. Or better yet..." Her focus shifted back to SAC Hunt. "Send in one of your guys."

"I would, but my team has been actively investigating Valdez for a while now. They've spoken to him and his people, been around his properties. Some have even questioned Valdez directly."

"We could find another detective or agent and put them under, sure," Cam chimed back in. "But that would take time."

It was Izzy's turn to shrug. "Okay. You said yourselves,

you've been after this guy for a while. A few more weeks won't hurt."

"Not us, no." A muscle in Riedell's jaw twitched. "But I've got three dead kids, and the longer Valdez breathes free air, that number's just going to keep rising. Not to mention all the drugs and weapons that will be passed around the streets of this city in that time. Or more importantly, the number of missing young women and girls we suspect were lost to the sick bastard's trafficking gig."

"Izzy, we understand your hesitation with this," Cam attempted to be the sound of reason once again. "But putting someone on the inside...getting them close enough to make a man like Valdez trust them...that sort of thing takes time. We're talking months. Sometimes even years. Now I'm not trying to guilt trip you into anything here. I promise I'm not. But I've personally spoken to a few of the families impacted by Valdez's evil doings, and I'm telling you...we've already waited far too long. The man needs to be stopped."

"I don't disagree." Izzy held the other woman's empathetic stare. "I just don't think Olly is the guy to stop him."

"Maybe not." Sgt. Riedell sat back in his chair. "But right now, your brother's our best option."

Her chest felt tight, and the nausea was growing stronger. "How do you know he'll even agree to work for you?"

"We don't." Hunt rested his hands on his narrow hips. "That's why we'd like you to be the one to talk him into it."

Forget the nausea, Izzy suddenly found herself struggling to catch her breath. "You just spent the last several minutes telling me how disgustingly dangerous Dante Valdez is. Now you're telling me you want me to talk my brother into getting close to the guy so he can record his confession to murder and...all the other stuff you say this man's done?"

"Yes." Cam's expression softened with understanding. "It's a big ask, we know. But this man has to be stopped, hopefully sooner rather than later."

It wasn't a big ask. It was massive. And even if Izzy wanted to play along with the whole crazy scheme...

"I haven't seen or spoken to my brother in over two years. I-I...I didn't even know he was in town." She swallowed the painful knot that admission created and went on. "How can you be so sure he'll even talk to me?"

"He nearly killed a man to protect you."

Looking up at the man still standing to her right, Izzy didn't bother asking how he knew about that. "Yes, Agent Hunt. He did. And his life has been nothing but jail, drugs, and heartache ever since. All because he wanted to help me. So to think he'd want to put himself in danger like that again simply because I asked him to..."

"That's all we're looking for here, Izzy." Cam's petite hand rested on Izzy's shoulder. "We're just asking you to try."

She considered this for a moment. "I don't even know where he's staying. Like I said, Olly never even called to let me know he was back in Denver."

Right on cue, Hunt held out a small piece of paper with an address scribbled across it in black ink. "This is where your brother's currently staying. It's a low-income housing unit. I'll give you two guesses as to who owns the building."

Izzy didn't need two guesses. She didn't need to *guess* at all. Dante Valdez owned the building where Olly was staying.

He worked for the guy and lived in an apartment owned

by him. It might not take much to get close enough for a taped confession...

"What if I did it?"

All three sets of eyes lasered in on her, but it was Hunt who spoke up first.

"What if you did what?"

"Is Valdez single?" Izzy didn't wait for an actual response. "If he is, you could use me. I could reconnect with Olly, make sure to put myself in a position to be introduced to Valdez...I flirt a little and try to get him to ask me out. You could fit me with the wire and camera. I entice him into taking me on a date...work him until I get what you need... You get your guy, and Olly stays safe."

"I appreciate the offer, Izzy, but no." Sgt. Riedell shot her idea down without hesitation. "It's too dangerous."

"You're willing to risk my brother's life to get what you want. Why not mine?"

"It's different."

"A life is a life, Sergeant."

From across the desk, Grady's boss stared her down. "I know what you're trying to do, and I get it. I also respect you for it. But it's not going to happen."

"What about you?" She looked over at Hunt. "You said the FBI's been after Valdez for a long time. Don't you have a say in the decision?"

"I do." The man's expression was as stiff as his neatly pressed suit. "And I agree with Sgt. Riedell. The whole reason we called you in here was to explain the situation in hopes that you'd convince your brother to help us. Not so you could use yourself as bait."

"Who does or doesn't put themselves in the line of fire shouldn't matter. What's important is the *results*. I'm telling you; I can get them."

"The offer is appreciated, but your request is denied."

When Izzy looked back at the man behind the desk, she realized any further argument would be futile. Riedell had made up his mind as had SAC Hunt.

"We understand your need to protect your brother," Cam rejoined the conversation. "But we've looked at this from every possible angle. Trust me when I say Olly is our best option. And if he is involved with Valdez's illegal dealings, I think it's safe to say your brother's in way over his head."

"Because you think I can convince him to go along with this crazy plan?" She met the other woman's gaze and held it.

"We're hoping you'll at least try."

Izzy's mind raced as she weighed her options. She loved her brother fiercely, and her loyalty to him was unwavering. She owed her life to Olly. He'd saved her from a danger so unthinkable it still haunted her dreams.

A detail she'd held close to the vest since that horrific night.

Riedell and the others know what happened. They practically said as much.

Her heart sunk to her toes. Did Grady know, too? Had he looked into her background after they first met?

If he did, he never said anything. Not that she should even be worried about that right now.

Glancing back down at the paper still clutched in her hand, she didn't recognize the street name, but that didn't matter. Olly was here, and she was absolutely going to pay him a visit. As for the other...

"I'll try." She lifted her head and took in the room. "But that's all I can do. I can't promise my brother will even talk to me, let alone agree to—"

"All we're asking is for you to try," Hunt cut her off.

The room fell into a focused silence, the weight of the task at hand settling over them. Eventually, Sgt. Riedell moved the rest of the meeting forward and the four present discussed plans, strategies, and Izzy was provided with additional pertinent information. All the while, her mind raced with questions and possibilities.

But one thing remained certain—she would go to great lengths to protect the only family she had left. Which meant doing everything she could to get Olly far away from Dante Valdez's corrupt world.

Izzy rose slowly to her feet. Sliding the thin strap of her purse back onto her shoulder, she gave each of the others a parting glance before muttering, "I'll let you know how it goes" just before walking out the door.

4

"Well there's an hour and a half of our lives we'll never get back." Grady held the door open for his partner and waited for him to pass.

"No kidding." Declan stepped over the threshold and into the lobby of their home away from home.

There were several districts within the DPD, but there wasn't any other department Grady would rather work in. Even if some days—like today—he and Dec felt as if they were chasing their tails.

"At least we got Torres."

Letting the door swing shut behind him, Grady walked with his partner through the tiled lobby, past the reception desk, and toward the set of stairs leading to their team's secured space.

"True." He swiped his ID, the telltale click of the metal lock disengaging letting him know he'd been granted access. "Just wish the asshole was willing to wire up so we could take down Valdez."

As long as the head of the snake was intact, the man's

sick and twisted business would continue slithering its way through Denver's streets.

"We'll get him," Declan assured him as they started up the stairs. "Just need to find another way in."

"Yeah, I know. Was hoping we'd found it with Valdez's ex, but..."

He didn't finish because he didn't need to. They'd just come from a visit with Dante Valdez's ex-wife and to say she was less than receptive to the idea of sharing anything about her time spent with the dickhead was a major understatement.

The woman seemed to dislike cops almost as much as she hated her former husband, so their entire conversation was very much one-sided. He and Declan had done their damnedest to make her see that by helping them, she'd be ridding herself of Valdez for good, but nothing they said seemed to matter.

"She's scared of him, you know," he pointed out the obvious to his partner.

"Picked up on that, too, did ya?" Declan shook his head in disgust. "Asshole probably put her through hell when they were still together."

"From what we know about Valdez, she's lucky she got out of their marriage alive."

The other man nodded. "And she knows if she talks to the cops, she's as good as dead."

"Yeah, she may be a piece of work, but she's not stupid." With Declan marching beside him, he made his way up the stairs to the precinct's second floor.

The open area contained the team's desks and their 'crime board' used to keep track of important details and players in whichever case they were working at the time. On the far end was their boss's office, and to the right was the staff break room, which preceded the hallway leading to the unit's interrogation rooms.

But when Grady turned the corner at the top of the stairs, he didn't see any of those things. All he saw was...

Izzy.

By some twist of fate, he nearly collided with the woman who'd haunted his dreams for the past two nights...or the past several months, if he was being completely honest with himself.

"Oh!" Her round eyes met his with a start. "Sorry."

"Whoa." Grady reached out a hand to steady her. "Where's the fire?"

"What? Oh." A nervous chuckle. "No fire. Just distracted, I guess."

Izzy attempted to brush off their near mishap, but Grady could tell something was wrong. Their time together may have been brief—and mostly sexual—but he knew her well enough to recognize when something was off.

"What's wrong?"

"Nothing. Just a jam-packed day, that's all."

The smile she wore was nowhere near genuine. Despite knowing he should, Grady couldn't let that shit go.

"Try again."

"Uh...I'll go fill Sarge in on what we found. Or rather, what we didn't find." Dec stepped around them, offering Izzy a quick greeting as he passed. "Good to see you again, Dr. Garcia."

"You, too, Detective." Another fake smile.

Waiting for his partner to be out of earshot, Grady let his hand drop back to his side and returned his full attention to the woman standing before him. "You look upset."

"It's nothing. Really."

Nice try, sweetheart.

"Iz—"

"Really, Grady. It's just been a day, and now I'm late for a meeting across town."

She was lying. Maybe not about being late for the meeting or having a rough day, but there was *something* the sexy doc wasn't telling him.

"You sure?" He slid his hands into his pockets to keep from reaching for her again. Lowering his voice, he added for her ears only, "You can still talk to me, you know."

A flicker of hesitation passed over her worried face. For a second, he thought she was actually going to open up to him. Instead Izzy's shoulders moved back, her chin lifting slightly with an obvious move to compose herself.

"I appreciate that, but I really do have to go."

Before he could protest further, she hastily excused herself and rushed down the stairs. Grady stood there, hands still in his pockets and heart sinking as he watched her disappear.

Needing answers, he moved further into the bullpen. Fellow detective Cole Archer was leaning against his desk, engrossed in a case file he was currently reading.

"Hey, Cole." Grady approached the other man, doing his best not to show his frustration.

Cole glanced up. "Hey, Thorne. How'd it go with Valdez's ex?"

"It didn't. Listen..." He stepped closer, keeping his voice low so the others wouldn't hear. "You know why Dr. Garcia was here?"

Setting the folder on the desk behind him, Cole crossed his arms in front of him casually. "No clue. She got here a while ago. Had a closed-door meeting with Riedell, Hunt, and Umbridge, then left."

Grady swung his gaze toward his boss's office in time to

see the FBI's SAC Jeremy Hunt and ADA Camille Umbridge walking out. The two were involved in what appeared to be a serious conversation, barely noticing Grady and the others as they made their way through the open space and down the stairs.

Izzy had a meeting with his boss, the FBI, and an ADA?

"Well that can't be good," he mumbled more to himself, rather than to his teammate. "And you have no idea why they were here?" *Or why Izzy was included in the meeting?*

Cole shook his head. "I'm not sure, man. Whatever it was, it looked serious."

Grady's frustration mounted. Unable to get the concern —and quite frankly, the *fear*—in Izzy's eyes out of his head, he started for his sergeant's office. As he walked past Declan's desk, his partner attempted to deter him from his mission.

"Hey, man. What's going on?"

"Not sure."

"You maybe wanna talk it out before you go barging into Sarge's office?"

"Nope." He kept walking.

With an unconcerned shrug, Declan mumbled, "Your funeral."

As his partner went back to whatever he was doing on his computer, Grady entered Riedell's private space uninvited.

"You got a minute?"

Closing the file he'd been studying, Sgt. Riedell glanced up from his desk, meeting Grady's intense gaze. "Come on in, Thorne. You and King get something useful from the wife?"

"She was a bust." He shook his head. "Valdez has her so conditioned she's too afraid to talk to us."

"We knew it was a long shot." The salt-and-pepper-haired man didn't sound surprised. "There something else?"

Grady took a seat in front of Riedell's desk and rested his elbows on his denim-covered thighs. "I know it's none of my business, but I was hoping you'd tell me why Dr. Garcia was here."

"You seem pretty invested in Dr. Garcia lately. First at that hostage situation and now this." With an almost knowing look, Riedell leaned back in his chair, his boss clasping his hands together before resting them in his lap. "There something I need to know about the two of you?"

Grady felt a pang of hurt, but not from the insinuation. No, his pain stemmed from the fact that, as of two days ago, there wasn't a damn thing between him and the gorgeous Dr. Garcia. But just because they were no longer sleeping together, that didn't mean he didn't still care.

"There's nothing going on between me and Garcia, Sarge," he replied firmly, his voice leaving no room for doubt. "But we are friends, and she just left here looking pretty upset. Then I see Hunt and Umbridge leaving right after, so I just wanted to check and make sure everything was okay."

His boss studied him for a moment longer before rising to his feet. "Not sure *okay* is the word I'd use, but there is something I need to fill the team in on. May as well tell you all together so I only have to say it once."

Ah, hell.

Grady prayed this wasn't about to be some sort of lecture on inter-office relationships. The last thing he needed was to be singled out in front of the men and women he worked with.

He mentally replayed all the moments he and Izzy had shared over the last few months, doing his best to recall any that could have caused an issue with work. But try as he might, nothing sprung to mind.

You were so careful. Izzy made sure of that.

It was true. They never went out in public together unless it was to meet up as a group from work. And when they engaged in those types of social events, he and Iz were always, *always* diligent about not giving off anything other than friendly co-worker vibes.

But that didn't mean they hadn't fucked up. Maybe the higher-ups that had been in that meeting had gotten word of his...relationship...with Izzy, and now she was in trouble. Or they both were.

That doesn't make sense. If the meeting were about a personnel issue, it would've been held in HR, not in Riedell's office.

No, there was something more at play here. Something involving their unit, the FBI, and the District Attorney's office. And whatever it was, it had obviously upset Izzy.

"Come on." His sergeant picked up the file folder he'd been staring at when Grady first walked in.

Rounding the edge of his desk, the serious man stepped past Grady and left the room. Following his lead, Grady left the office and rejoined the rest of his team in the bullpen.

"Listen up." Riedell stood near their nearly filled case board and waited. With his hands in his pockets, he addressed the group as a whole. "I'm sure you're all wondering why Hunt, Umbridge, and Dr. Garcia were here." A few mumbled agreements floated through the air, but the added sound died down quickly. "As you know, Torres flipped on Valdez, but he's still refusing to wire up for us."

"Hunt wanting to send one of us in?" Cole glanced around at the others before his piercing blue gaze returned to Riedell's. "Boss, a UC operation's going to take a while to get going."

"Especially with someone as sharp as Dante Valdez," Kim agreed.

Sitting at the desk across from Cole's, her blonde hair was pulled back in her signature ponytail. She and Cole had been partners since well before Grady joined the DPD, and from everything he'd seen, they were as solid as partners could be.

Like the rest of them, Kim's intelligent baby blues were filled with intense curiosity as the team waited for more. Thankfully, they didn't have to wait long.

"As most of you saw, I just had a meeting with SAC Hunt and ADA Umbridge," Sgt. Riedell commented. "You probably noticed Dr. Garcia joined us, and I'm sure there are questions. So here it is." He walked over to the case board, pulled two photos from the file in his hands. Clipping them to the board for all to see, he turned to face the group. "This is Oliver Garcia. He's an ex-con who did time a while back for breaking and entering, as well as aggravated assault. According to Hunt, Garcia drifts in and out of town every so often. Something his sister confirmed. Right now, Garcia is back in, and he works for Dante Valdez."

Grady stared at the two images. One was a mugshot showing a young, unapologetic kid from several years prior. The other a recent and somewhat grainy surveillance photo.

"Garcia?" He'd picked up on that little fact right away. "Don't suppose he's any relation to—"

"Oliver is Dr. Garcia's older brother," Riedell answered the question before it was fully posed.

Brother?

Izzy never mentioned anything about having a sibling. Of course, the fact that he's an ex-con who worked for the man they were trying like hell to take down may have had something to do with that.

Not that Grady would've cared. Izzy was her own person, and Grady knew better than most not to judge someone based on their familial relations.

"What kind of work does Garcia do for Valdez?" The question came from Blake Jacobs who was standing near his own desk.

The one across from him was currently empty, the team still down one since Jacobs' partner moved across the country three weeks prior.

"That's still unknown," Riedell answered Jacobs. "What we do know is Oliver, or Olly as his sister calls him, has an in with Valdez, and we're hoping to use it to bypass the usual undercover set-up. Because Archer's right. A UC op like the one we're trying to put together inside Valdez's world would take a long damn time, and there are too many innocent lives at risk."

"Not sure I'd call Juan Gomez or the other two Los Reyes stiffs innocent," King quipped.

"Regardless"—Riedell continued—"time is not on our side, so we're gonna play this one a little unconventionally."

"Meaning?" Grady listened intently, his gut becoming tighter and tighter the longer his boss spoke.

An unconventional UC op involving the FBI, ADA, and Izzy? This can't be good.

"Meaning, Dr. Garcia has agreed to talk to her brother on our behalf. She's going to explain the situation, and with any luck, he'll agree to be our CI for the purposes of this case. I won't know for sure until I hear back from Isobel, but the FBI and DA's office is hopeful—as am I—that she can convince her brother to get us the evidence needed for an arrest and conviction."

"And if she can't?" Grady looked at his boss, whose seasoned eyes met his without hesitation.

"If this lead falls through, we'll have no choice but to start back at square one."

"Or wait for the next Los Reyes corpse to make an appearance," Cole muttered half-teasingly. "Of course, I guess if it comes to that, we can always try to get his next hitman for hire to flip."

Riedell turned to Cole. "Let's hope Dr. Garcia comes through before that happens. These kids may not be innocent, but they're still just kids."

"Kids who were dealt a shitty hand and ended up in the wrong crowds." Kim stood a few feet from the board, arms crossed at her chest as she studied it closely. "I mean, Jacobs is right. These guys are bad news, but most of them probably felt they didn't have a choice when they joined the Los Reyes. Hell, they may not have *had* a choice but to get in with a gang."

"Join or die." Cole nodded solemnly. "Some of the harshest ones lay it out like that for their recruits. You're either in, or—"

"You're dead," Declan finished for their teammate. "I've seen it happen before. The members pressure neighborhood kids until they fold, using threats against them, their family. Friends. Guys like Valdez will do just about anything to keep their business growing."

"And the kids do whatever they have to in order to survive." Kim kept her line of sight in the board's direction.

"Which leaves us here, spinning our wheels while guys like Valdez get away with murder. Literally."

"Yeah, well he won't be a free man long." Riedell took in the entire room. "Not if I can help it. So let's keep going. Pound the pavement, knock on doors...do whatever you've gotta do to find something we can use. In the meantime, I'll keep in touch with Dr. Garcia about her brother."

One question was clawing its way to the forefront of Grady's whirling mind. Unsure if he really wanted the answer, it was something he needed to know regardless.

"Did Iz...er...Dr. Garcia know about her brother's connection to Valdez?"

"She claims she didn't even know he was back in town. For what it's worth, I believe her," Riedell put Grady's mind at ease. "According to what she shared, the two haven't spoken or seen each other in over two years."

Kim didn't appear convinced. "But she thinks she can convince him to work with us on this?"

"Dr. Garcia didn't promise anything aside from bringing her brother up to speed. She does that, the choice is out of her hands. No one can force the guy to sign up as our informant." Their boss shifted his stance, waiting for further comments that never came. "Look, I didn't say the plan was foolproof, but for now, it's all we have."

"You said she was going to talk to her brother tonight." Like before, Kim posed her next question to Riedell. "If she didn't know he was in town, how will she know where to find him?"

"Hunt's team was able to track down the address where the brother's been staying. Dr. Garcia is going by there tonight to hopefully talk with her brother. With any luck, she'll have him back in here to meet with us first thing in the morning. Until then, we keep working this thing as if Olly Garcia doesn't exist."

"Makes sense." Cole pushed himself off his desk and slowly walked over to his chair. "If she can't talk him into playing along, it may as well be true." When the man's feisty partner shot him a disapproving glare, he belatedly added, "Obviously the guy *exists*. I just meant for the purpose of solving this case."

As the pair began a hushed debate over the detective's poor choice of words—which really wasn't much of a debate given that Kim was a master at putting Cole in his place—the rest of them went on about their jobs.

Riedell returned to his office. Blake began typing away on his keyboard. Declan joined Kim near the whiteboard. And Grady...

Grady wasn't really paying much attention to any of that. He was too busy staring at Oliver "Olly" Garcia's frozen image.

Looking to be in his mid-to-late thirties, the guy appeared to stand right around six feet. Comparing the two photos, it was obvious Izzy's brother had beefed up during his time away.

Even beneath his well-worn clothes, Grady could tell Garcia's arms, chest, and legs were much bigger and more defined than when he'd been arrested years before. The guy's dark, shaggy hair was almost the exact same shade as Izzy's, but it was his eyes that really drew Grady's attention.

Though they weren't crystal clear in the surveillance image Riedell had posted, the mugshot showed eyes the same shape and color as Izzy's.

I can't believe she never told me she had a brother.

Sure, they hadn't divulged a ton of personal details. Another one of her no-strings rules. But Grady had pretty much been an open book as far as anything she *did* want to know.

Despite her being so close-lipped when it came to herself.

The longer Grady stared at that damn picture, the more he began to realize he knew very little about the mysterious Dr. Garcia.

That was about to change, though. Starting now.

Turning his back on the board, Grady walked over to where his partner still stood. Keeping his voice down, he asked, "You feel like a quick visit to the FBI?"

"The FBI?" Declan's dark eyes slid to the closed office door behind Grady and back again. "What are you thinking?"

"I'm thinking I want to know where Olly Garcia lives."

"You heard Sarge. Izzy's gonna try to talk to him later."

"And I plan on being there when she does."

The other man hesitated in his agreement, the internal war happening inside him damn near visible to the naked eye.

"Relax, Dec. I know things got a little heated at the hostage scene a while back, but I'm good to go. You heard what Boss said. This guy's an ex-con who works for a piece of shit like Valdez. Not to mention, Izzy hasn't seen or spoken to him in over two years."

A little heated was an understatement. During the aforementioned hostage situation, Grady had nearly lost his shit when Izzy walked straight into the hands of their HT, or hostage taker.

Luckily for all involved, the situation resolved itself without anyone being injured.

"You want eyes on her in case their sibling reunion goes sideways," his partner read his mind.

"Damn right I do. And you should, too." He rubbed the taut muscles at the back of his neck. "I've just got a bad feeling about this, and I know I won't rest tonight not knowing for sure that she got in and out of wherever this guy lives unscathed."

For the next handful of seconds, Declan didn't say a word. Instead, he just stood there, staring back at Grady as if he were trying to solve some age-old mystery.

Just when Grady was about to tell his partner to forget it, Declan opened the top drawer of his desk and grabbed his holster and gun. Standing up, he clipped the weapon to his belt and pushed in his chair.

"Let's go."

"Yeah?"

With a hand to his shoulder, his partner gave him a solid squeeze. "I know you care about Izzy, and so do I. If your gut's screaming that this thing with her brother could go sideways, then she should have someone there watching her back. May as well be us, right?"

One corner of Grady's lips curved, and he was reminded yet again how lucky he was to have made this place his home. Pulling his keys from his jeans, he gave Declan a nod and said, "I'll drive."

5

Izzy stood outside the dilapidated apartment building, her heart racing with a mixture of anticipation and anxiety. She gripped the edges of her coat tighter, the chill of the night seeping through to her skin.

She hadn't seen her older brother in so long, their estrangement leaving a painful, gaping hole in her life she hadn't been able to fill. Aside from Olly finding his way back to the man he used to be, there wasn't anything Izzy wanted more than for the two of them to reconcile.

It's too late, Iz. Too much time has passed.

The same doubting voice she'd been forced to listen to for years rang through her mind. But Izzy refused to give it life, her experience and training teaching her that, for some, it was never too late.

It was that thought that had fueled her decision to put on her coat and shoes, get into her car, and drive to a part of Denver she'd never seen. At eight o'clock at night, no less.

She would have been here sooner, but like she'd told Grady when the two nearly ran into each other hours earlier, she really did have an afternoon meeting across town.

He thought you were lying.

Izzy's gut felt tight just thinking about Grady and the others knowing about her past. She hadn't wanted *anyone* to know. Especially him.

But after today—after this—he would. That is, if he didn't already.

She glanced up at the building once more. Coming here was probably a massive mistake. One she'd come close to avoiding by nearly crawling under the covers of her plush bed and pretending like the meeting with the FBI and the DA's office never happened.

But every time she closed her eyes, she saw that picture of Olly at Valdez's warehouse, and she couldn't stand the thought of him being anywhere near a man like that. Let alone work for him.

So here she was. Fueled by her love for her brother and a desire to keep him safe, she'd followed her GPS system to the run-down place before her.

Taking a deep breath, Izzy walked across the shadowed street, equally relieved and creeped out when she didn't see another soul in sight. Climbing the worn-out stairs leading to a set of even worse-looking wooden, double doors, she looked for a buzzer but found none.

She reached for one of the large metal handles and pulled the heavy door open. Almost instantly, she was struck with a wave of humid, musty air that reminded her of an old, damp basement.

Her heart sank when the lobby came into view.

Stained tiled floors. A wall of metal mailboxes, half of which no longer had doors. Trash was scattered about, and the elevator directly in front of her had a strip of yellow caution tape that appeared to have been put into place a long while ago.

Oh, Olly.

Shifting course, Izzy headed up the set of narrow wooden stairs. Each step creating a symphony of creaks and moans straight out of the scariest horror movie imaginable.

She reached the top, her heart saddened by the state of the second-floor hallway. Much like the lobby, its floors—albeit carpeted—were marred with stains. The walls cracked and discolored from years of neglect.

The overhead lights gave her direction as she navigated her way to her destination, but a flickering bulb at the very end of the hallway screamed for someone to replace it.

Izzy spotted the apartment she was searching for and came to a stop before it. Filling her lungs with a steely breath, she lifted a fist and rapped her knuckles against it.

The sound echoed through the empty hallway.

Filled with nervous energy, Izzy lowered her hand back to her side and shifted her stance from foot-to-foot. Several seconds passed with no response, so she raised her hand a second time preparing to knock again. But before she could make contact a second time, the sound of a chain lock sliding free was followed by a deadbolt disengaging.

Her heart pounded an unforgiving rhythm against her ribs. Izzy's breaths became shallow, and suddenly she found it difficult to breathe.

The door creaked open. After a torturously slow reveal, she found herself staring back into a set of eyes she'd missed dearly. Olly's hardened face softened with a look of pure surprise.

"Izzy?"

His voice sounded rougher than she remembered, and

there was a hint of caution hiding within his deep tone that wasn't there the last time they'd spoken.

Her brother's six-foot frame was bulkier than before, his muscles sculpted and toned in a way that made her think he spent several hours a week at the gym. His dark hair falling in a shaggy disarray.

The lines of worry etched across his forehead deepened, as if he couldn't believe she stood there before him. Round hazel eyes, once filled with mischief and laughter, now carried a hint of sorrow. Shadows that spoke of life's burdens marred the delicate skin beneath his gaze.

"Hey, Olly." She placed her hands in the oversized pockets of her coat, for no other reason than she wasn't sure what to do with them.

"Wha...what are you doing here?"

"I was about to ask you the same thing." A small smile lifted her lips, her pulse a fast and steady staccato of nerves. "Can I come in?"

After a moment's hesitation, he glanced up and down the hallway, almost as if he were afraid of someone seeing them together. Though it broke her heart to know he had to take time to ponder her request, she understood why he would.

"I won't stay long," she offered, her own voice betraying a mix of sadness and pain. "I just..."

She what...came here to try to convince him to risk his life by working with the Feds to catch a killer? Not exactly the heartwarming reunion she'd been hoping for. But before she could come up with a believable reason for showing up unannounced when he hadn't even told her he'd returned to Denver, Olly shifted to the side and made room for her to pass.

"Thanks." Izzy stepped into the dimly lit home. Standing

in the tiny living room, she did a quick—and hopefully indiscernible—visual of where her brother had been staying.

Dull, peeling wallpaper, carpet that looked older than her, furniture that was functional but extremely dated, dishes piled in the sink...

This is all my fault.

The door shut behind her, pulling Izzy's focus back to where it needed to be.

"How did you, uh...how did you find me?" Olly came to a stop next to where she still stood.

She'd never lied to her brother before, and she wasn't going to start now. "The FBI gave me your address."

"FBI?" Alarm flashed across his confused gaze. "Why the hell are the Feds looking for me?"

"They aren't looking for you, Ol. They..." Izzy turned toward the living room and sighed. "Maybe we should sit down for this conversation."

Motioning toward the worn and faded couch, he told her, "Knock yourself out." As he followed her the few feet it took to get there, Olly added a sarcastic, "I'd offer you something to drink, but I'm guessing your tastes are a little more refined than mine."

"Please don't do that." Izzy lowered herself onto the thinly padded cushion.

"Do what?"

"You hide behind sarcasm and humor so people don't see your pain."

"You shrinkin' me now, Sis?" He plopped down into the mismatched chair resting against the room's west wall. "You should know by now that shit doesn't work on me."

"I'm just expressing what I can see. And those walls of

yours..." She swallowed. "They're the same ones I see every time I look into a mirror."

Olly's hard lines softened, and for the first time since opening the door, he almost looked like the brother she remembered. Almost.

"Why are you here, Iz? And before you ask; I still don't do drugs, I rarely drink, and I haven't had so much as a parking ticket since before I left Denver the last time. Oh, and I have a good job."

"Working for Dante Valdez?" She watched him closely.

His brows furrowed. "How did you...oh, right. The Feds." He lifted a leg and rested it over the other knee. "What is it this time? Because whatever it is they think I've done, I swear to you, I haven't—"

"It's not like that." She rushed for reassurance. "Your boss..." Izzy blew out a breath and went for it. "Olly, Dante Valdez is a very bad man. He's suspected to have given orders for at least three murders, all members of a local Mexican gang very much active here in the city. A gang Valdez has known ties to."

"I just told you I'm not doing anything illegal."

"I don't think you are. But your boss is. And it's bad, Olly. We're talking drugs, weapons...human trafficking. The Feds think he's in deep with all that stuff, and if you're working for him—"

"There's nothing they can pin on me, because I'm not in any of that shit. I load and drive trucks, Iz. I get a call; I go to a warehouse in the south part of town, load the boxes waiting for transport, then I deliver them to wherever he sends me. That's it."

"No one thinks you're involved in Valdez's illegal dealings." When he shot her a look of disbelief, she amended her statement by saying, "Fine, *I* don't believe you're involved. But I know you, Olly. I know the kind of person you are, and there's no way you'd—"

"You sure about that?" Another sarcastic quip. "I mean, we haven't seen or spoken to each other in a long damn time."

"Yeah? And whose fault is that?" Izzy regretted the snarky question the instant it left her lips. "I'm sorry. That was uncalled for."

"Doesn't mean it isn't true."

A stretch of time passed between them before she finally broke the silence. "I don't care if it's been two years or two hundred." She stared back at him. "I know you, Ol. That's how I know you'd never, *ever* go along with trafficking of any kind. Especially young girls."

"Damn right, I wouldn't."

The flash of anger flaring behind his hazel gaze sent a rush of guilt racing through her. But before she could apologize, Olly did his best to dismiss her.

"Thanks for coming by, Iz, but you really shouldn't be here. It's not...safe."

"Why? Because of your boss?"

"No, because it's a shit hole building in a shitty part of town. A woman who looks like you, dressed in your fancy suit and expensive heels... You're a walking target for guys who live around here. Hell, I'd be surprised if your car's still where you left it."

"I'll take my chances."

With a shake of his head, Olly pushed himself to his feet and marched into the less-than-modest kitchen. Opening the small refrigerator, he pulled out a bottle of water and lifted it as if to ask if she wanted it. When she shook her head, he twisted off the small plastic lid and tossed it into the overflowing trash.

It hit the corner of an empty cereal box and fell to the floor, but her brother ignored it and chugged half of the bottle's contents in one long gulp. His guarded stare found hers once more as he wiped his mouth with the back of his forearm.

"Okay, let's have it. What do the Feds want you to talk me into?"

God, I hate how hardened he's become.

"I had a meeting a few hours ago with the head of DPD's Major Crimes unit, the FBI, and one of the city's ADAs." *Just tell him.* "They've been investigating your boss for a while now, but they haven't been able to get enough to lock him up. In the course of their investigation, they discovered you and that you're my brother."

"So they're trying to use you to get to me, that about right?"

That's exactly right.

"They want you to wear a wire to work. Try to get Valdez on tape admitting he ordered the execution of three Los Reyes members. If you can get him to talk about the other nefarious businesses they believe he's running, even better. But the murders would put him away for life and end his trafficking business for good."

Laughter echoed off the decades-old walls. "Boy, they don't ask for much, do they?"

"I know it's a lot—"

"Uh, you think?" He took another swig, clearly upset by her revelation. "Valdez didn't get to the top by being stupid. The guy sniffs even the slightest hint of a set-up, he'll kill me. And I don't mean that metaphorically."

"I know you don't." Izzy swallowed a giant knot in her throat. "I also know how dangerous it would be for you. That's why I tried talking them out of it."

"Really?" The lines on his face smoothed slightly. "You did that?"

"Of course I did." Izzy stood and went to him. "Look I know I messed things up for you back then, but you're still my brother." Tears welled in her eyes, but she did her best to keep them at bay. "Nothing I say or do will ever make up for what happened, but I love you, and I will *always* do whatever I can to protect you."

He was quiet for a stretch, his unreadable gaze searching hers for...something. She wasn't quite sure what, but then...

"Ah hell, Iz." He ran a hand through his unkempt hair. "We've talked about this a million times. I thought you finally understood. What happened back then wasn't your fault. It was *his*. Well, his and that bitch of a wife."

"But—"

"Damn it, Iz! There are no buts!" He actually sounded angry then. "That bastard would have raped you if I hadn't done what I did. And if he got away with it once, he would've done it again. And again, and again, and again. You know I'm right."

The flashbacks loomed, but Izzy used the coping mechanisms she'd learned a lifetime ago to help push them back below the surface. A tear escaped, but she swiped it away before it could get too far.

"I know. And I'm incredibly grateful you showed up when you did. But at the same time, if you hadn't, you never would've gone to prison, and you wouldn't be—"

"A total loser?" His brow arched expectantly.

She sighed. "I was going to say you wouldn't be so unhappy."

"Yeah, well." Olly shrugged, his eyes flickering with a mix of guilt and regret. "That's life, right? Not everyone is meant to have a happy ever after. No matter how much *you* want them to."

"Olly..."

Her heart ached for her brother's lost dreams and potential. He deserved more than this. More than a life in the shadows.

"It's okay. Really. I made peace with it a long time ago. You should, too."

Make peace with the fact that her brother—a man who, as a kid himself, had sacrificed his own future to save hers?

Never gonna happen.

"You can still have your happy ending, Olly. You said it yourself; you have a steady job and you've been staying out of trouble... It's a great start."

"A job the FBI is apparently hell bent on screwing up." Another shake of his head. "I don't get it. If they think Valdez is such a bad guy, why isn't he behind bars?"

"Like you said, Valdez is smart. And the Feds need more solid proof of his involvement before they can obtain an arrest warrant." She licked her dry lips before adding, "You can always say no. If it were up to me, I wouldn't even be here asking."

"If you don't want me to do it, why bother coming by?"

"Honesty I thought if you knew what your boss was doing on the side, you'd quit and find employment elsewhere. Someplace safe without fear of getting a bullet to the back of the head because you made your boss mad."

Tilting his head slightly, Olly studied her with an assessing glance. "You really think Valdez is doing what they say, don't you?"

"I do." She nodded. "Listen, I know you don't have a lot of trust when it comes to law enforcement, and I understand why. But the people I work with...they're the real deal, Olly.

Sergeant Riedell runs Denver's Major Crimes unit. He and his team are working the three murder cases tied to Valdez. I'm friends with his team, and I can promise you they're the good guys."

"Friends" sounded wrong as it had fallen from her lips, but she and Olly had only just reunited. Izzy was *not* about to delve into the whole casual sex relationship she'd just ended with Grady. Not when they had more pressing issues to tend to.

"Even if that's true"—Olly finally spoke again—"you said the Feds are going after Valdez."

"It's a joint investigation. Major Crimes is working with one of the local FBI units. I haven't personally worked with them yet, but I know several people who have, including Sergeant Riedell and his team. And everything I've ever heard about SAC Hunt's unit is good. Better than good, actually. They have the highest solve rate in the entire Denver Bureau. That's gotta say something, right?"

"I don't know, maybe." A slight shrug. Olly was quiet for a moment, presumably taking everything in that she'd shared. But then, "Is that the only reason you came here tonight?"

His voice sounded off with that last question. Small, almost vulnerable. Very unlike the Olly she knew and loved.

Is it possible? Could I have been wrong about him all this time? Was I wrong about...everything?

For the past seventeen years, she'd carried around a massive dose of soul-crushing guilt. For so many things.

Izzy felt guilty for what had happened to her parents. She woke up every morning blaming herself for Olly's trouble with the law. Sometimes on those particularly hard days and nights, the little girl in her still questioned if she'd said or done something to lead on the man who'd attacked her that fateful night.

But now...

I thought you finally understood. What happened back then wasn't your fault. It was his.

She looked up at her brother with renewed vision. A professional, clinically assessing vision. And what she found there nearly brought her to her knees.

He isn't looking at you with hate or resentment. There's no animosity or blame reflected in his intense stare. In fact, the only things Izzy did find there were regret and...

Love.

"I came by because I learned my brother was in town, and I wanted to see him," she finally answered him. Izzy paused before she whispered a low, "I've missed you, Olly. More than I can ever say."

"I've missed you, too." His throat worked a hard swallow. "A lot."

The admission caused her damaged heart to swell and tears to form in her eyes. "Really?"

"You're my sister, Iz. I know I've been a shitty brother, but—"

"No, you haven't." She moved closer to him. "You just had a lot handed to you at a very young age."

"I wasn't the only one. Yet here you are, a successful psychiatrist working with the heads of law enforcement."

It was a conversation they'd debated ad nauseum, and Izzy sensed this wasn't the time to rehash unwinnable arguments. So instead, she went with, "I wish you would've called when you first got back into town."

An uncomfortable silence blanketed them before she heard a soft and surprising, "Figured it was best if I didn't."

"What?" She frowned. "Why on earth would you think that?"

He shrugged again. "Didn't want my shit falling into your world, I guess."

"Oh, Olly. You're my *brother*. My world *is* your world. At least, it could be if you'd let it."

"I know you believe that, but—"

"It's true."

A few seconds passed before she picked up a small pad of paper and pen from the scratched and dented end table positioned between the couch and chair. Scribbling her number and address, she ripped the top sheet off and held it out for him.

"That's the address to the precinct. I'll be there at eight in the morning, along with Sergeant Riedell and SAC Hunt. If you decide you want to listen to what they have to say, come. If not, my address and phone number are below it. Those haven't changed since you were here last." When he didn't take the offering, she added, "Help the FBI or don't. The choice is one hundred percent yours. Either way, I'd really like it if we could stay in touch. If you want, that is."

Her brother stared at the paper in her hand, and still he made no move to accept it.

Come on, Ol. Let's use what time we have left to be a family again. Please, just take the paper.

He didn't take it.

Accepting the fact that he might just need some time to work through everything she'd intrusively dropped in his lap, Izzy carefully set it on the coffee table beside her. Returning the pad and pen to their rightful place on the end table, she went back to him and sighed.

She'd told him it was his choice to help the authorities,

and it was. Just like it was up to him to want to repair what had been broken between them so long ago.

Not wanting to push too much too quickly, Izzy stood directly in front of him. After a few trepidatious starts, she wrapped her arms around her brother and held him close.

He didn't hug her back right away, but the moment he did...

"I love you, Olly."

His hold tightened, and she felt a sweet kiss on the top of her head followed by a soft, "Love you, too, Sis."

Twin tears fell from her closed lids, but she didn't even care. She and her brother still had a lot to work through, but this was as close to a start as they'd had since he was sent off to prison.

"Not to sound like a dick, but you really do need to get out of here." He pulled away far too soon. "It's getting late, and nothing good happens after dark in this neighborhood."

"Walk me to my car?"

"Let me grab my jacket."

Feeling lighter than she had in forever, Izzy started for the door when it swung open with a bang. Standing in the doorway was a man who radiated danger. Tall and meaty, his cold eyes roamed over her, his gaze settling on Olly with a sense of ownership.

"What the hell, man?" Olly slid his arms through his jacket sleeves as he marched toward the uninvited guest. "I told your ass last time you need to knock."

"Boss has a new job for you." The man grunted. His voice was rough and laced with an undercurrent of menace. "He wants to see you first thing in the morning."

Izzy's heart sank, knowing the big jerk was talking about

Dante Valdez. God, she hated that Olly was entangled in the evil man's web.

"You couldn't have texted that shit?" Olly didn't sound intimidated by the man in the least. "Can't you see I have company?"

That makes one of us.

"Boss wanted to make sure you got the message." His cold, shiver-inducing focus returned to her. "Who's this?"

Olly glanced her way before answering, "Just a chick I know."

Normally Izzy would balk at being called a chick, but in this particular instance, she wasn't going to complain. It was clear Olly didn't want to announce her as his sister, so she went along with it.

Plastering a polite smile on her face, she stepped toward the unknown man and held out her hand. "I'm Bella." A nickname her dad sometimes used. "It's nice to meet you."

The man's emotionless stare pierced through her as he ignored her outstretched hand. Turning his attention back to Olly, he reiterated his message with an air of authority. "Be at the warehouse at seven-thirty sharp. And don't be late."

"Whatever, man. I'll be there. But the next time you come here, you'd better fucking knock."

Unfazed by Olly's vague threat, the man shot them both a final intimidating glare before turning around and walking away. Left in the uneasy silence, Izzy raced to the door and shut it.

"Let me guess." She faced her brother once more. "One of Valdez's men?"

"You need to go." Olly's voice was stern. "I'll call as soon as whatever job he has for me in the morning is finished. And..." He filled his lungs before blowing out a breath. "If your buddies at the DPD and FBI still want to meet, we can figure out a time. But you heard what Tony said. If I don't make that job in the morning—"

"It's fine. If you decide to listen to what Riedell and Hunt have to say, just let me know. We can always plan to meet up later in the day." She put a hand to his arm. "Just promise me you'll be careful."

"You know me." The wink and hint of a smirk were the first real signs of the old Olly she'd seen since knocking on his door.

"Call me when you're finished doing whatever Valdez needs you to do. I'll keep my phone on me at all times so I don't miss you."

"See that? I let you in my place, and you're already trying to boss me around."

Flashing her brother a genuine smile, Izzy rose to her tiptoes and kissed his rugged cheek. "I love you, Olly. Don't forget to call, okay?"

"If I do forget, you'll probably just show up at my door anyway."

The teasing tone in his voice was a soothing balm to her soul. "Damn right, I would."

"Come on." He opened the door and waited for her to step into the hall. "I'll walk you out."

As she made her way through the decrepit hallway and down the creaky stairs, Izzy felt lighter than she had in years. It wasn't as if there weren't still cracks in her relationship with Olly, but this was the first time in their entire adult lives she remembered feeling...*hope*.

Now she just had to make sure he didn't get himself killed.

6

Grady watched from the shadows as Izzy and a man he recognized as her brother hugged goodbye on the building's front steps. He waited not wanting to cause a scene. Especially if the giant bastard he'd seen exit the building a few minutes before had somehow circled back to lurk around.

Sitting behind the wheel of his non-descript car—courtesy of the DPD's overflow lot—Grady had taken several pictures of the muscle-bound man when he'd first arrived. He'd then sent them to Declan, who'd ran the image through the department's facial rec system.

By the time the man left, Grady knew pretty much all there was to know about Anthony George Fitch, A.K.A. Tony the Tank.

The thirty-four-year-old douchebag had a rap sheet as long as Grady's arms. Everything from petty theft to illegal drugs, including weapons possession and aggravated assault.

But the most interesting detail in the guy's jacket was his association with Valdez.

On paper, Fitch was Valdez's head of security. If Valdez

needed to be somewhere, Fitch drove him. If there was a public event at which Valdez needed to make an appearance, Fitch was his unofficial bodyguard.

The two were practically attached at the hip, and the fact that he'd just gone into the same apartment building where Olly Garcia lived couldn't be a coincidence. But right now, Grady's focus was on Izzy, and making sure she was okay.

From what he could see, it appeared as if she was.

Grady kept his eyes on her as she looked both ways before crossing the street. Parked two spots up on the opposite side of the road, he got out and half-jogged to catch up to her.

"Hey." He blew out a breath as he came to a stop behind her. "Fancy meeting you here."

Izzy's small cry of surprise caught in her throat as she spun around. At the same time, she raised her fist as if to strike out at him, and it was then that Grady noticed the keys strategically placed between her folded knuckles.

"Easy there, Doc." He put his hands up to show he meant her no harm. "It's just me."

"Grady?" Her gorgeous face twisted into a rapid-fire mixture of shock, fear, confusion, and anger.

It was safe to say, that last one was what drove her to smack him square in the chest with the palm of her keyless hand.

"Didn't we *just* have a discussion about you sneaking up on people like that?"

Damn she's cute when she's pissed.

"I literally jogged from all the way down there." He tried not to smile. "Figured you would've heard me coming. Nice move with the keys, by the way. Smart."

"What?" She glanced down at her other hand, the keys still locked tight in her fist. "Oh. Sorry."

"Don't be. It's nice to know you're ready and willing to defend yourself if you had to."

The glow from the streetlamps made it possible to see the tiny twitch in her lips. But just when he thought she might offer him an honest-to-goodness smile, her brows scrunched together and she took a step back. "You're changing the subject and avoiding my question. What are you doing here?"

"Waiting for you."

"Me? Why?" Izzy frowned. "And how did you even know where I'd be?"

"Sarge filled us in on your brother's connection to Valdez. He said you agreed to talk to him about helping with the case, and I wanted to make sure you were safe."

"Oh. That's actually...really sweet." She tucked a lock of hair behind her ear.

"I take it things went well with your brother?"

At the mention of Olly, Izzy's features softened at the mention of her only sibling. "They did, actually. Better than I expected, to be honest."

"I'm glad." He really was. "He agree to help with the case?"

"He's considering it. I gave him the precinct's address, but he may not show. I told him the choice was his." Worry marred her otherwise flawless features. "I think I was making real progress with him, but then this guy showed up, and he told Olly their boss has some big job planned for first thing in the morning."

Grady pictured the man he'd seen go in and out of the building minutes earlier.

"Tall, mean looking, big wall of muscles?"

She nodded slowly.

"Guy's name is Tony Fitch," he shared. "He's Valdez's heavy hitter."

Surprise flickered in her widened gaze. "You know him?"

I know enough.

"I was watching the place from inside my car. Guy looked off, so I snapped a pic and sent it to Declan. He got a hit using facial rec."

"Well he's a peach, let me tell ya." Izzy crossed her arms at her chest. "Jerk just barged right into Olly's apartment like he owned the place."

Grady's fists tightened at his sides. An involuntary move brought on by the thought of a man like Fitch being anywhere near her.

"What did he want?"

"He didn't give specifics. Just that Valdez needs Olly for a job first thing tomorrow. Which means I'll have to let your sergeant know we need to move our meeting to later in the day."

"Fitch say what the job was?"

Izzy shook her head. "He never actually used Valdez's name, either. But I think that's because I was there."

"He say anything to you while he was in there"

"Not a word." Another negative gesture. "In fact, I introduced myself, and he just kept on talking to Olly as if I wasn't there."

"You gave the bastard your name?" The question fell from his lips with a growl. "Why the hell would you—"

"I said my name was Bella," she explained. "It's what my dad used to call me. When Fitch asked Olly who I was, he said I was just some chick he knew. I figured if that were true, I probably would've acted like everything was fine, so…"

"You introduced yourself but gave him a name you don't

normally use, but one you'd most likely answer to." Grady finished for her. "Quick thinking."

"I do have my moments, you know."

His lips curved into a sideways grin. "I know. I just hate the idea of you being anywhere near those guys."

Visibly rankled, Izzy uncrossed her arms and shot him an angry glare. "One of those *guys* is my brother, Grady."

Well, hell. "I wasn't talking about your brother, Iz." *Although if he's working for a guy like Valdez...* "To be honest, I hate that Riedell drug you into any of this in the first place."

His response must have appeased her concern because her narrowed gaze softened and the anger that had been present in her defensive tone vanished.

"You don't have to worry about me, Grady. I'm not..." The tip of her tongue swiped a quick line across her lips. "I'm not your responsibility."

Not his...

"See now, that's where you're wrong." Taking a broad step toward her, he locked his eyes onto her and did his best to make her understand. "Just because you broke things off the other day doesn't mean I stopped caring. We were friends before the mind-blowing sex, remember?" *Fucking phenomenal sex.* "As far as I'm concerned, that's never gonna change. So if I think there's a chance you could be in trouble, I'm going to be there to watch your back." For good measure he added a belated, "Whether you like it or not."

Face flushed, Izzy's gaze deepened. The pulse point at the side of her neck beating faster than before.

"I still care about you, too." A whispered confession. "And I understand and appreciate your concern, but as you can see, I'm perfectly fi—"

The telltale sound of a bullet whizzing past registered a millisecond before the window beside Izzy shattered.

"Get down!"

Grady threw his upper body over Izzy's, forcing her down to the pavement. The move was rough but necessary, just like the Glock 19 he'd just pulled from the leather holster at his hip.

"Are you okay?" He held his gun at the ready, his right arm moving left to right in a smooth and precise motion.

"I-I'm okay." Her voice shook with fear, but at least she hadn't been injured. "What was that?"

"Someone just took a shot at us."

And they'd come damn close to hitting her.

Rage firing through every nerve ending in his body, Grady kept his head on a constant swivel as he yanked his phone from his pocket and called it in. After giving the emergency operator his name, badge number, and a brief run-down, he requested units be sent to their location and ended the call.

He shoved the phone back into his jeans and considered their options.

You need to move. You have to get her someplace safe in case the son of a bitch tries again.

Knowing they were sitting ducks if they stayed put, he quickly came up with a plan to hopefully keep them *both* as safe as possible until back-up arrived.

"Is your car unlocked?"

"Y-yes."

"Okay, good. As soon as I say go, I want you to get to the other side of the car as quickly as you can. But stay low, got it?"

"O-okay." A frantic nod.

"When we get over there, I want you to open the back door, climb inside, and lay as far down on the floorboard as you can. Do you understand?"

"Fast and low, open the door, get inside, lay down." Her fearful but determined gaze met his with a hunched nod. "Got it."

If the situation wasn't so dire, her abbreviated recap would have made him smile.

Damn, she's cool under pressure.

Keeping an arm and one-half of his torso over her back, Grady scanned the entire area for the person behind the attempted assassination. "Be ready to move in three... two...*now!*"

He removed himself from Izzy's hunched form and she took off as instructed. With his gun at the ready and his gaze alert and focused, he followed her closely as the two made their way around the car's front bumper.

Keeping his eyes peeled for the threat, he continued covering her as best as he could while she opened the back passenger-side door and hurried inside.

"Keep the doors shut and keep your head down," he barked.

Izzy's worried gaze met his from over her shoulder. "What about you?"

"Don't worry about me. You just do as I say and stay down."

Grady could tell she didn't like that answer, but there was only a second's worth of hesitation passed before she gave him a jerky nod and squeezed her way down to the floorboard.

That's my girl.

Careful to make sure her feet were cleared, Grady pushed the door shut and spun around. He leaned against the car's smooth metal and waited for a second attack.

Thankfully one never came.

Within minutes, the entire area was swarming with

patrol units. A few curious neighbors also joined in the excitement, the small group studying the disruptive activity from behind the portable barricades as if they were trying to figure out what the hell happened.

That's what I want to know.

As soon as the officers on scene gave him the all-clear, he opened the door and assisted Izzy as she exited the vehicle. The minute she joined him on the sidewalk, Grady's first thought was to make sure she truly was okay.

"You good?" With his hands on her shoulders in a gentle hold, he did a quick head-to-toe scan of her body. "You're not hurt, are you?"

"I'm fine." Those big eyes of hers searched his for answers he wished like hell he possessed. "Did someone really try to shoot us?"

Not us, sweetheart. You.

Despite having no tangible proof, Grady's gut screamed that she'd been the shooter's target. But since he had no way of knowing for sure, he kept that hypothesis to himself.

Still somewhat shaken, Izzy turned and looked across the street, toward her brother's building. When she spotted him amongst the crowd, the two made eye contact, and she gave him a slight nod and a half-wave.

Grady watched the man closely for any signs he may have been behind the attack. But even from across the street, he could see the worry the other man held for his sister. The guy also looked beyond pissed.

This wasn't him.

"I should go over there and let him know I'm okay."

She stepped one foot off the curb, he reached out to stop her. "Wait." His fingers wrapped around her wrist in a strong yet gentle hold.

Izzy halted her forward movements and looked back at him. "What? You said it was safe."

"From the shooter, yeah. It most likely is."

"Then what's the problem?"

"Your brother could have tried to come over here himself, but he didn't."

"So?"

"So my guess is, he's keeping his distance in case Valdez has people watching."

He could see the wheels turning in that intelligent brain of hers. It didn't take long for her to reach his same level of understanding.

"You think Valdez was behind this?"

"I think we have to assume that until we're proven otherwise."

"If it *was* him, and he's trying to somehow test Olly..." A slight pause preceded her response. "If that's what's going on, and I go over there..."

"You could blow his cover before he ever gets the chance to wire up."

Once again, Izzy's forlorn gaze traveled the distance between her and her brother. But she stepped back up onto the sidewalk and stood by Grady's side.

Right where she belongs.

The unexpected thought took him by surprise, especially given where they were and what had just taken place. This wasn't the time or place to be thinking about that shit. Only...

It's not shit. It's...Izzy. And she was more than just a thought. She was...

Mine.

"Grady!"

Both he and Izzy turned their heads to see Sgt. Riedell

marching toward them. From the look on the man's face, he was as happy about the situation as was Grady.

"What the hell happened?" His boss's swift steps and long strides carried his lean form to where they stood.

Releasing the hold he still had on her tiny wrist, Grady spoke as he led Riedell and Izzy around the trunk to the other side of the car. "Someone took a shot at us." He pointed to the quarter-sized hole in the center of the spider-webbed glass. "Once the scene was secure, I did a search and found what looks to be a slug from a twenty-two."

"You thinking long gun?" his boss asked Grady's opinion.

"That or a long rifle pistol." Grady moved closer, pointing out the light, almost white circle surrounding the small hole. "You can see the pulverization of the glass surrounding the point of impact." For Izzy's benefit, he added, "That's due to the speed at which the bullet was traveling."

The entire window had shattered, but the design of the safety glass kept it otherwise intact.

"And you two didn't see anything before the shot was taken?"

"That's a negative, Boss." Grady shook his head. "Patrol's been canvassing the area, but so far there haven't been any signs of the shooter. Of course, the neighbors aren't talking."

"Let me guess. No one heard or saw anything?"

"Exactly."

"I still can't believe this happened." Izzy's soft voice reached his ears. "If we'd been standing an inch or two in the other direction..."

There was no need for her to finish the sentence. They all knew what would've happened if that had been the scenario.

I almost lost her.

"Someone just happens to take a shot at you right after you visit your estranged brother?" A muscle in Riedell's jaw bulged. "No way that's a coincidence."

"Agreed." Grady stared back at his boss with a nod.

"So what happens now?"

Both men turned to face Izzy who looked far too pale for Grady's liking. "Now, I'm going to get you out of here and someplace safe."

"Like where?" Her dark brows furrowed.

"You can stay with me." When her eyes widened, he added, "I'll take the couch, but I don't want you to be alone tonight. Not after this."

"I agree." His sergeant backed him up. "Until we know for sure who the shooter was and whether you were his target, you need to lay low."

"I appreciate the thought, Sergeant. Really, I do. But I also have a job to do, and people are counting on me to do it. And I won't be run out of my own home by some drug dealer with an ego trip."

Sliding his intense stare her way, Grady told Izzy point blank, "If that bullet was meant for you, there's a good chance there could be more headed your way."

"Thorne's right." His boss concurred. "Can't do your job if you're dead."

No one could ever accuse Riedell of being a sugar-coater, and right now the man's bluntness was exactly what Izzy needed to hear.

"Fine. I'll agree to the protective detail, but it's going to be at my house." She looked at Grady. "Nothing against your apartment. It's just my home office is there, my computer, files…it makes more sense to just have you stay with me, rather than the other way around."

"Done."

Well that was easier than expected. But there was still one more condition...

"My brother also needs protection."

"He'll have it," Grady's boss vowed. "The rest of the team and I are going to make a show of going across the street and knocking on doors. We need to see if anyone's willing to talk, but that will also give me an excuse to introduce myself to your brother and explain how things are going to work. His neighbors see me at his door, they'll think I'm questioning him like we are everyone else."

"That's...really smart." Izzy nodded. "What about tomorrow? What's the plan after tonight?"

Rather than answer her directly, Riedell looked to Grady with a gruff, "We need all hands on deck with this one."

"But Boss, you just said you wanted her under my protection."

"I said she should stay at your place and lay low. I'll have a uniform posted at your apartment twenty-four-seven. That way you can do your job and Izzy stays safe."

Grady wasn't too happy with his boss's plan. He much preferred to be the one watching over Izzy. But the detective in him knew this course of action made the most sense for all involved.

So rather than stand in the street debating, he said, "If you don't need anything else from me..."

"Go. I'll let you know if we find anything we can use."

"Copy that." To Izzy, Grady said, "Come on. Let's get you out of here."

As they walked to his car—the palm of his hand resting protectively against her lower back as they went—Grady did his best not to let her see the murderous rage brewing inside him.

Someone had taken a shot at her tonight. Someone

who'd intended on seeing her dead. And when he found the person responsible...

You're fucking dead.

SHADOWS CROSSED DANTE VALDEZ'S HARDENED FACE AS HE leaned back in his leather chair and tapped his fingers rhythmically against the mahogany desk. Tony, his right-hand-man and confidant, stood in front of him.

"Tell me what happened."

"I went to Garcia's apartment like you asked." Tony's dark gaze remained locked with his.

Dante's gaze bore into his trusted friend's, his voice cutting through the heavy silence. "And?"

"I told him about the meet. But there was a woman there. Pretty, dark hair. Sharp eyes. Not exactly the kind of woman I would've expected to find hanging around a guy like Olly."

"You know who she is?"

"Olly said she was just some chick he knew, but I could tell there was more to it than that."

"You get her name?"

"She introduced herself as Bella. That's all I got, but..." Tony hesitated, which was very much out of character for the brute of a man.

"Spit it out."

"After I left, I circled around. Cut through a nearby alley, parked the car, and walked in the shadows. I waited down the block until she came out. Was going to follow her. Get an address, run a background. You know the drill."

"I do, indeed."

"Anyway, the woman was about to get into her car when

this other dude comes running up to her. Tall. Bald. Bearded." Tony took a breath. "At first, I thought he was going to mug her or pull a carjacking or some shit. But then they started talking, and it was obvious they knew each other. They seemed close. Friends maybe. Possibly more."

"Is there a point you're trying to make?"

"The guy she was talking with is a cop." Tony finally got there.

Interesting. "You know this how?"

"The guy looked and moved like a pig, so I took a picture and sent it to your source for confirmation. The man is Detective Grady Thorne. He has an apartment on the north end of the city."

"And the woman?"

"Dr. Isobel Garcia."

"Garcia?"

Tony nodded. "Olly's sister who also happens to be a forensic psychiatrist on the DPD's payroll."

So Olly had a sister who was in bed with the cops. Not only that, he'd lied to Tony about who she really was.

"Did you take care of the problem?"

"Tried to, but a damn stray cat came out of nowhere. Fucking thing rubbed up against my leg right as I pulled the trigger."

"So you missed." It wasn't something that happened very often.

"Yeah, I fucking missed." Tony ran a hand over his dark hair. "They took cover, but I saw the asshole get on his phone as they moved out of my line of sight. I knew he was probably reporting the shooting to his cop buddies, so I got the hell out of there."

"Cutting your losses isn't always an easy choice to make,

but that doesn't mean it isn't sometimes necessary. You did the right thing by coming to me with this."

"Thanks, Dante. If it weren't for that damn cat—"

"It's over and in the past." Dante waved the man's excuse away. "We need to focus on the future."

"What are you thinking?"

"I think there are three rats in our house that need to be exterminated." He stared into his man's eyes to ensure he understood the unspoken order.

Tony's jaw tightened, his loyalty to Dante etched in every line of his face. "Consider it done, Boss."

Dante leaned back in his chair once more, his gaze focused on the world beyond the walls of his fortress. The weight of impending danger settled upon his shoulders. A burden he'd grown accustomed to bearing.

Peace came with the knowledge that Tony would take care of things. Just as he had every other time an infestation threatened what Dante had spent his life building.

Because no one messed with his livelihood and lived to tell about it.

7

Izzy stood in her living room, the only light coming from a small table lamp in the far corner of the room. The moon hung low, casting a soft glow over the surrounding mountains, giving the scene an ethereal touch.

"You have a beautiful home." Grady's deep voice rumbled as he stepped up beside her.

The familiar scent of male spice and something uniquely his filled the air around her, creating a sense of security she only ever felt with him.

Only Grady.

"Thank you." She took the offered cup of steaming hot tea he'd taken the time to brew.

Putting the porcelain mug to her lips, she sipped the amber liquid carefully to avoid getting burned. The action nearly made her laugh as she compared it to the way she'd been living her life.

Careful. Cautious. Never letting anyone too close for fear of being burned.

It had worked splendidly—until now. But a change had

been brewing for some time, now. One she'd fought like hell to ignore.

Hard to ignore when he's standing right beside you.

Her inner voice wasn't wrong. The craziness of the last few days had offered ample proof of that.

Everything about her was changing. Probably had been since the day she first met the sexy beast of a man. She could still remember their first introduction as if it were yesterday.

The way her breath had caught in her lungs when those piercing eyes of his met hers. The electric pulse shooting through her at their first shared handshake. The way her insides had contracted, and her body had ached at that first panty-dropping smile.

But the one thing that stood out from all of that was the unexplainable ease at which Izzy felt when Grady was there. It made no sense whatsoever, even for someone of her profession. It simply...was.

Grady was sweet. Sexy. Ferociously protective of those he loved, and the most incredible lover she'd ever had. But most importantly...

He makes me feel safe.

Safe. Treasured. Cherished.

Though she'd done her best to ignore it, Izzy could no longer deny what was happening between them. What had started as a casual fling somehow turned into something more. And no matter how hard she fought it or how many times she told herself it wasn't what she wanted, Izzy finally understood.

I'm falling for him.

Truth be told, she was probably already there. And though the timing was less than ideal, Izzy couldn't ignore the fact that she'd come damn close to dying tonight. They both had. And now...

All I can think about is what if I'd died without ever allowing myself to love?

It was ridiculous and highly inappropriate given the circumstances, but Olly was safe and so was she. For now, at least.

It was late, and nothing more could be done from her end until morning anyway. And being locked away in her own home with the very man who'd risked his life for her mere hours before, Izzy realized there may never be a perfect time for what she needed to do.

After taking another slow sip of her tea, she turned away from the window and set the mug on the end table next to her cherished chaise.

"Olly's safe, Iz," he muttered low, presumably misreading her silence as worry for her brother.

She *was* worried for Olly. How could she not be? But in that particular moment, that wasn't at the forefront of her mind.

Maybe it should have been, or maybe...

"I know." Izzy faced the man who made her heart race. "He called while you were in the shower."

She'd taken one herself as soon as they'd gotten to her place, using the brief respite as a chance to regain her composure and move past the night's terrifying turn of events.

"Then what's got you looking like you're contemplating life's greatest mysteries?"

"I don't know." She shrugged. "Maybe I am, in a way."

"Yeah? Wanna share what's rolling around in that incredible head of yours?"

Did she? Normally her answer would be an instant and

resounding no. But this time, Izzy found herself *wanting* to tell him. Found herself wanting to do all sorts of things she'd never allowed herself in the past.

As they stood in the room's soft glow, Izzy found herself wanting to hold him...and let him hold her. She wanted to finally let go of her deepest, darkest secrets, and lose herself in the heat and passion only this man could create.

Only him. Only Grady.

Maybe it was adrenaline or her tearful and unexpected reunion with Olly. Her cycle was slated to start soon, so it could simply be hormones run amuck.

Or—and this was a very real possibility—she could be looking for a plausible excuse that didn't exist and was a mistake on the grandest of scales. But it didn't matter.

Izzy was tired of living half a life. Tired of hiding in the shadows of the world, and tired of always being alone. After all, how could she expect Olly to put himself out there and let others in if she wasn't willing to do those things herself?

Before she could chicken out, Izzy closed the remaining distance between them in a few purposeful strides. She stopped directly in front of him.

"Iz?"

"You want to know what I'm thinking?" She waited for his nod and then, "How 'bout I show you, instead?"

Izzy leaned up and pressed her lips to his. Grady stiffened beneath her touch, clearly surprised by her invitation. Thankfully it didn't take long for him to catch up.

Their kiss was a collision of desire and longing. It started slow, a gentle exploration of each other's mouths, but soon escalated into a passionate tangle of tongues and urgent need.

Grady's hands slid down Izzy's body, tracing the contours of her curves through the thin fabric of her shorts and tank sleep set. Each touch, each caress, fueled the fire that raged between them. Their need for one another threatening to consume them both.

Breaking the kiss, Grady pulled his head back just far enough to look into her eyes. "You've had a helluva day, Iz. Emotions are running high, and you're probably still coming down from a massive adrenaline rush—"

"I know what I'm doing, Grady." She needed to make that point crystal clear.

"The other day we stood in that parking garage, and you told me you were done. You said we were done." A strong hand rubbed across his salt-and-pepper beard. "I want nothing more than to be with you again, but I can't...I *won't*...take advantage of you. Not like this."

Always protecting me. Even from myself.

Her heart swelled, her body aching for the love she felt for this man. It was a love she could no longer deny.

"I appreciate you looking out for me, Grady." She stared up at him. "But this isn't what you think."

"Then what is it? Because from where I'm standing, it feels a lot like a woman who nearly died needing the reminder that she didn't. I get that need, Iz. To feel alive after a close call like the one you just experienced. Trust me on that, sweetheart. And I'm more than happy to make that happen for you, but—"

"I love you." The blurted confession was unplanned and much louder than intended. But it was out there now, and she couldn't take the words back.

Shock left his mouth slack jawed and his eyes as big as saucers. "What did you just say?"

Can't lie your way out of this one, Iz. Go on. Tell him again.

"I said I love you." A hard swallow. "I'm...*in* love with

you. And I know because I've never felt this way about anyone before."

"I...uh..."

"You don't have to say anything. Really. I'm not fishing for platitudes or false promises. I don't even know if you feel even close to the same way, and that's okay. After tonight, I realized...I didn't want another moment to pass without you knowing."

Still staring back at her as if she'd just asked him to calculate some rocket-science-level equation, he cleared his throat and said, "But the other day, in the parking garage. You said—"

"I lied."

"You lied." He continued staring. "Which part did you lie about?"

"All of it. When I told you I didn't want more. That I had no interest in a serious relationship. It was all a lie designed to cover up the soul-crushing fear I've been living with since I was fifteen. Which is a whole other story, and one you absolutely deserve to hear. Right now, I don't..." She licked her lips again. "I don't want to talk, Grady."

"What do you want, Isobel?"

Her heart rate spiked at the sound of his entrancing voice uttering her given name. "I want you to make love to me, Grady." Izzy lifted a hand to his cheek, his beard tickling her palm as she brushed her thumb back and forth in a gentle motion. "Please. Tell me I'm not alone in this."

"You're not alone, baby." He pulled her close. "I love you, too, Iz. So fucking much. I think I have from the moment we met. And as long as there's breath still left in my lungs, you'll never be alone again."

Izzy wasn't sure who moved first, and she didn't care. All she knew was one second, she was staring up in to the eyes that had changed her entire world when she wasn't looking. The next, Grady was sweeping her into his arms and carrying her into her bedroom.

They reached the bed, and she expected him to place her on the mattress. He didn't. Instead, Grady set her down onto her feet, his hands never leaving her until he was sure she was steady.

Izzy's heart pounded against her ribs, the anticipation of what was about to happen the greatest foreplay she'd ever experienced. It wasn't like this was their first time having sex. Not even close.

But it would be the first time Izzy had truly made *love* with anyone. And she couldn't wait.

She reached for Grady, but he surprised her by taking a step back, keeping himself just out of reach. The intensity in his gaze made her pulse quicken and she watched with bated breath as he slowly unbuttoned his light blue dress shirt.

His sculpted chest was revealed, and though she'd touched him countless times before, Izzy's fingers itched to reach out for him. But she waited.

She'd dropped a bomb of mega proportions on him back in the living room, and now the ball was in his court. As far as Izzy was concerned, the reins were his to use and she was simply along for the ride.

And what a ride it's going to be.

Letting him remain in control, she watched and waited as he slid the shirt from his broad shoulders. The soft material fell to the floor, but neither paid it any attention.

Grady's eyes, smoldering with passion, locked onto hers. Izzy felt her body respond instantly, the yearning for his touch surging through her. Their connection was undeniable, a force that drew them together from that very first meeting.

She'd just been too blind to believe she deserved it.

But after seeing Olly again, after fighting for him to see his worth, Izzy realized she should take her own advice. Life was short. Tonight was a very real reminder of that, and she was done living with her head in the sand while everyone else around her thrived.

I want this. I deserve this. And there's absolutely nothing wrong with that.

Unable to resist any longer, Izzy reached out and ran her fingertips along the defined lines of Grady's chest and abs. Those muscles flexed, and she loved how his body responded to her touch.

Grady let out a low groan, his eyes darkening with desire as he shed the rest of his clothes. Izzy's breath caught in her throat, the sight of his naked form, powerful and unyielding, making her ache as if she had never had him before.

His impressive erection jutted toward her, and though she knew what it felt to have him buried deep inside her, Izzy felt her knees begin to tremble with unbridled need.

Without a word, he moved closer, invading her space in order to begin undressing her. Helping him along, Izzy took over yanking the tank top up over her head while he pushed her shorts down the length of her thighs.

He tossed the shorts aside, the thin material landing in a pile near the tank she'd dropped somewhere over to the side. Rising up once more, Grady went for the the front clasp of her lacy bra, releasing it with an expert flick of his thumb and forefinger.

Izzy's breath hitched, her ample breasts spilling free as the delicate scrap of material slid off her shoulders under the guidance of his strong, calloused hands.

"So beautiful." The compliment rumbled through her. She knew this moment was different for her. But now...

He feels it, too.

Grady reached for her, his palms filling with the perky globes. The room echoed with Izzy's moans, and she closed her eyes and arched into his touch.

Using his thumbs and forefingers, he playfully tweaked her nipples as his mouth took hers in a slow, devouring kiss. With their tongues swirling in an erotic dance, they each used the precious moment to explore.

She was familiar with nearly every inch of his muscular form, but like everything else about this moment, Izzy felt as if she were touching him for the very first time.

In a way, she was.

Grady swiftly lifted her into his arms a second time, carefully laying her in the center of the bed. The room was bathed in a soft, golden light coming from the half-opened curtains hanging on the windows across the room.

The mattress dipped from his weight as he crawled onto the bed beside her. Grady's eyes never left hers as his hands traced nearly every inch of her exposed skin.

It was slow. Torturous. His touch setting her ablaze as he stared down at her with a hungry gaze.

When he was finished with the pulse-spiking tease, Grady shifted himself so his body covered hers. The skin-on-skin contact sent a jolt of electricity straight to her core. She could feel his desire, hard and urgent, pressing against her thigh.

Their kisses grew more fervent, their tongues entwining with a desperate hunger. Together their bodies moved in perfect synchrony, a passionate dance that left them both breathless.

And he wasn't even inside her yet.

Grady's hand trailed down Izzy's body, teasing her again with more feather-light touches that drove her wild with need. A soft gasp escaped Izzy's lips as he reached the apex of her thighs.

She was hot and wet, her body ready and willing for him to take her, but Grady continued taking his time in the most delicious of ways.

His fingers explored her most intimate folds. Like every other second of this pivotal moment in time, he took his time playing her body as if it had been designed solely for his pleasure.

He circled her clit with his thumb, sending shockwaves of pleasure coursing through her body. Izzy's back arched, her nails digging into Grady's back as she surrendered herself completely to the sensations he was evoking within her.

Unable to bear the ache any longer, Izzy lifted her hips and pressed her core against his steely rod. Taking the hint —thank God—Grady reached between their bodies and positioned himself at her entrance.

Slowly, he began pushing inside her. The feel of being filled by him, of their bodies joining together as one, was almost overwhelming. Izzy's breath hitched as he began to move, each thrust driving them both closer to the edge of ecstasy.

"God, Iz," Grady moaned.

"I know." She smiled up at him. "I feel it, too."

The corners of his lips curved, her whispered admission clearly bringing him joy. Their bodies moved in a rhythm as old as time, each thrust pushing them further into a world of pure pleasure.

Their moans mingled in the air, a symphony of desire that echoed through the room. The intensity built with every stroke, with every passionate kiss, until they were both on the precipice of release.

In the final moments of their union, Izzy and Grady held on to each other, their bodies writhing in the throes of passion. As they reached their peak, their cries of pleasure filled the room, mingling with the sound of their pounding hearts.

And even when their bodies were depleted, they clung to each other. Their bodies trembling with the intensity of their unbreakable connection.

As their breathing slowed, Grady gently withdrew from her sensitive core, collapsing on the bed beside where Izzy lay. Turning on her side, their bodies became a tangle of limbs and shared heat as they savored the afterglow of their lovemaking.

Unlike the other times they'd been together, Izzy felt no urgency to make a quick escape. In fact, as their gazes remained locked in a look that spoke volumes, she realized she never wanted to leave.

His arms. Their shared bed. His life.

How this man managed to worm his way past her impenetrable defenses would forever be a mystery. But as she lay in Grady's arms, Izzy knew she'd found something truly special—a connection that transcended the boundaries of physical desire.

Suddenly, surprisingly, she couldn't wait to explore every facet of their love together. As she eventually let her lids fall closed, Izzy knew she would never be the same.

8

GRADY PACED his unit's bullpen while he waited for Izzy and her brother to arrive.

Last night had been a game changer of epic proportions. Hours later—he was still trying to wrap his mind around the fact that Isobel Garcia—the most anti-commitment woman he'd ever had the pleasure of knowing—was in love with him.

A woman who never let anyone in, had confessed to being in love with him. And he couldn't be happier about that if he tried.

She'd been right when she'd said they still had a lot left to discuss, and he'd planned on doing just that over the breakfast he intended to make. But those plans changed when he was called in to work a new lead that, like so many others on this case, had yielded squat.

By the time he and Dec had chased their tails all over town, it was already mid-morning. He'd hated leaving her, especially when she'd looked so beautiful—so peaceful—lying naked and asleep beneath the covers.

But duty called, so he'd waited until the uniformed officer taking his place had arrived. After he briefed the experienced officer on the situation, Grady gave the other man a stern directive to contact him if he even felt something was off.

For Izzy, he left her a quick note before departing for work. Now here he was, acting like a nervous Nellie as he waited for her to show.

"You're gonna wear a hole in the tile if you don't sit your ass down and relax." The comment came from Declan, who was messing with a rubber band while sitting at his desk.

"Hard to relax when I know Izzy's in a vulnerable position that could put her in the line of fire."

The rest of the team was out working other angles that were case-related, and Riedell was in his office with the door shut. The man had been on and off the phone ever since he and Dec had been back.

"She's riding here in a police cruiser with her very own cop as a bodyguard," Declan pointed out. It was clear the guy thought he was worrying for nothing.

"I get that, but I was standing right next to her when that bullet damn near took her from me," Grady shot back.

He realized his blunder the minute the anger-fueled words escaped.

"Took her from you?" A slow grin spread across Dec's face. "I knew you were holding out on me."

"I wasn't..." Grady sighed and plopped his ass in the chair across from his partner. Licking his lips, he tried to explain in a way the other man would understand. "Fine. I'll tell you, but you have to swear not to utter a single fucking word about it to Iz. Got it?"

"Dude, I'm not a complete asshole."

"I know, it's just..." Another sigh. "Do you remember

that night a few months back when we all went out for drinks to celebrate closing the Schellenberger case?"

It had been a particularly gruesome murder-for-hire scheme where the husband had hired someone to torture his wife to death. The husband was a doctor and really fucking smart, so it took the team longer than usual to find the evidence needed to put the bastard away for life. But, as was the way with his team, they'd done their due diligence and eventually got their man.

"I remember." Declan nodded. "We went to Sin. Drank some. Danced a little. It was a good night."

Sure as hell was.

"I took Izzy home that night. We agreed to keep things casual, which I thought was all I wanted. So did she. But…"

"It became more."

Grady nodded. "A whole lot more."

"That's great, man." His partner smiled. "Really. I'm happy for you."

"Thanks." He almost felt himself blush. "The thing is, Izzy's a very private person. I don't want something said that could offend or embarrass her."

"I get it, man. I won't say anything."

"Funny thing is, she actually broke things off the other day."

"That explains why I had to put up with your cranky ass for two days."

"Yeah, sorry about that." Grady grinned. "This whole time she's been preaching how she doesn't do commitments and all that, but then last night after we got to her house…I don't know. It was like the shooting opened her eyes or something, because the next thing I know, she's telling me she's in love with me."

Dec nearly spit out the drink of coffee he'd just sipped

between his lips. "In love?" The other man coughed and sputtered. "Well that's..."

"Fucking awesome." Grady smiled wide.

"I take it the feeling's mutual?"

"Oh, yeah. I mean, I agreed to the no-strings deal at first because I thought the same thing. I've never been in love before. Never been with a woman who made me think of the future and kids and all that."

"And now?"

"Now..." Grady's heart swelled at the thought of building a future with Izzy. "Now I can't wait to see where this thing with her is gonna go."

"I know that feeling. Still feel that every single day with Skye. Not a better feeling in the world than knowing you have a good woman who loves you."

No, he couldn't imagine there was.

"She doesn't make it easy for people to get close to her."

Declan sat back in his chair and linked his fingers behind his head. "Not surprised, given what happened to her and her brother when they were kids."

Grady swung his gaze to his partner's. "What do you mean?" He frowned. "What happened when they were kids?"

"Oh, shit. I'm sorry, man. I just assumed you knew."

"Knew what?"

Rather than answer the question, Declan asked one of his own. "You really don't know?"

"If I knew, do you think I'd be asking?"

"Sorry, I just...I guess I figured you'd already looked her up since you guys had that whole friends-with-benefits thing going on."

"I thought about it," he confessed. "In the end, I decided

I wanted to do things the old-fashioned way. Let her reveal facts about herself as she and I got to know each other better."

"Well, I'm guessing by your reaction to my comment, she never got into any of it with you."

"Considering I don't know what it is, no. She never told me." Grady rested his elbows on the table and shot Declan a look that said he'd better start talking.

"Shit, man. Now I don't know if I should tell you—"

"For fuck's sake, Dec. Will you just spill it already?"

Declan opened his mouth—presumably to reveal whatever the hell he wasn't saying—but their conversation got cut short when the rest of the team emerged from the stairs.

He and his partner shared a look, and damn if Grady wasn't going to have to wait to hear whatever it was Dec knew about Izzy and her brother.

"We'll talk later," Dec muttered before turning to the others. "Get anything useful?"

"Not a damn thing." Jacobs pulled his gun and holster from his belt and placed it in his desk drawer roughly.

They were all feeling the frustration from not being any further along on a shooting involving two of their own. And Izzy was one of them...whether she realized it or not.

"I did get a call from the lab," Kim announced. "Ballistics came back on the bullet recovered from Dr. Garcia's car. As we thought, it was a twenty-two. No prints or viable DNA, which is no big surprise."

"So we've got nothing." Grady shoved himself to his feet, unable to sit still a moment longer.

"We'll find the asshole who took a shot at you, Thorne." Cole's serious gaze found his.

"They weren't shooting at me." He set that record

straight. "That bullet was meant for Izzy. I'd bet my paycheck on it."

"You think Valdez knows she's trying to talk her brother into working UC for us?"

"I don't know what he knows."

He just wanted the bastard stopped, once and for all.

Riedell's door opened, and their boss addressed the team as a whole. "That was Sgt. Wright from downstairs. Dr. Garcia and her brother are on their way up now."

About damn time.

Grady turned to see Izzy and Olly cresting the top of the staircase. Their eyes met, and his heart did that whole skipping a beat thing it always did when she entered a room.

Dressed in a casual look of jeans, laced boots, and a simple black sweater, the woman looked good enough to eat.

Focus, dickhead.

"Dr. Garcia, thanks for coming," Riedell greeted them.

"Of course." She smiled at his boss. "Everyone, this is Oliver, or Olly, as I call him. Olly, this is…everyone."

Grady went straight to the man and held out his hand. "Grady Thorne."

"Olly." The man's handshake was solid. "Izzy told me a little about you on the ride here."

His gaze slid to the woman in question, who looked completely unapologetic for having been talking about him with her brother.

God, I love her.

A month ago, that thought would've scared him shitless. Hell, a *week* ago, it would've sent him running with his tail between his legs. But now…

I'm never letting her go.

"Hey." She smiled up at him.

"Hey, yourself."

"I think we'll all be more comfortable if we move this into the conference room," Riedell announced. Motioning for the hallway on the man's left, the group began filtering in that direction.

Once inside the modest meeting space, the team began choosing seats around the rectangular table centered in the room. Grady chose a seat near the front, positioning himself next to Izzy who took the chair to her brother's left.

"I've asked Dr. Garcia and her brother to come here so we can make sure we're all on the same page with everything," Riedell started. "Hunt and Umbridge were supposed to join us, but they were called away for something unrelated to this case. I told them I'd fill them in once we're finished here. Dr. Garcia, the floor is yours."

"I think at this point, you all can start calling me Izzy." She flashed a small smile to his boss and the rest of the room.

With a nod, Riedell acknowledged her request and moved on. "Okay, Izzy. If you'd like to begin..."

Grady turned to her, wondering why their boss was giving her the room. It didn't take long for him to figure it out.

"Your boss asked me and my brother here so Olly could tell you himself what he knows about Dante Valdez. But before he does, there are a few things I'd like to lay on the table, just to get it out of the way so there won't be any confusion or misguided suspicions."

"Misguided suspicions?" Grady's brow furrowed as he searched her gaze for more.

"Pretty sure she's talking about me," Olly commented casually.

"As a matter of fact..." Izzy turned to Riedell with a question in her gorgeous eyes. "Is it ready?"

"The remote's right there." His boss pointed to a small remote positioned near the corner of the table.

Picking it up, Izzy pressed a button to power up the large flat screen mounted high on the wall for all to see. As she filled them all in on Olly's background, the images on the screen changed to correlate with what was being discussed.

"When I was nine and Olly was twelve, our parents were killed by a drunk driver. They were both only children, and our grandparents on both sides were either already dead, in a nursing home, or unable to be found. We were thrown into the system, bounced around from foster home to foster home for the next several years. Olly aged out when he was seventeen, but since I was younger, I was forced to stay while the family we'd been living with kicked Olly out on the streets."

"Damn." Grady turned to Olly who simply shrugged with a *it is what it is* expression.

"Long story short," Izzy continued, "the husband in that home was a sick prick who liked playing with teenage girls."

Ah, fuck.

Grady's spine stiffened, his stomach churning with an instant and fierce nausea. Suddenly he found himself not wanting to hear any more of what the woman he loved had to say. But she went on, not giving him the option to escape.

"Before anyone gets too upset, I wasn't raped."

"Thank fuck for that," Grady bit out, not caring that everyone in the room could hear.

"But I almost was." Izzy swallowed, the pain in her eyes breaking his heart. "When I was fifteen, the man who was in charge of caring for us snuck into my room one night. He'd been putting off weird vibes for a few weeks before that, and just that night, he'd made some off-handed comment about how I was finally starting to 'fill out' my sweaters more. His wife just stood there, washing dishes as if her husband hadn't just come on to me. After, I was talking to Olly on the phone, and I mentioned it. Two hours later, my foster father snuck into my room and climbed into bed with me."

"The son of a bitch was on top of her," Olly seethed. "Holding her down when I came in through the window."

Son of a—

"Please tell me you killed the sick fuck." Jacobs looked almost as infuriated as Grady felt.

"Unfortunately, no. But I did beat the shit out of him."

"That's why you were arrested," Grady surmised.

Olly nodded. "Bastard sexually assaults my sister, and I end up serving four years."

"That's rough, man." Cole shared a look with the other man. "I'm sorry."

A stretch of thick silence filled the next few seconds, but it was broken when Kim offered Izzy's brother a few kind words.

"Your sister's damn lucky you showed up when you did." The sweet blonde stared across the table at Olly. "Just sucks that you had to face jail time while her attacker got off Scot-Free."

"Yeah, well...that family had money. Lots of it. The only solace I have is knowing they divorced a year later, and he had a massive stroke six months after that. Dickhead's been sipping his meals through a straw and drooling all over his bib ever since."

"Guess Karma really is a bitch," Declan groused.

"Asshole got off easy, if you ask me." Olly glanced his sister's way, the look of fierce anger and regret impossible to miss.

"What about the wife?" Kim asked. "If she knew what the husband was up to—"

"Oh, she knew," Izzy confirmed. "But they had a lot of powerful friends and even more cash. Their team of lawyers would've put O.J.'s dream team to shame. Meanwhile, Olly had to put his life in the hands of an overworked, underpaid public defender who did the bare minimum to qualify as having given his client a full and fair defense."

"So you get sent off to prison for defending your sister from a rapist while the actual offender and the woman who covered for him walk away free and clear."

"What can I say?" Olly's lips curved in a sarcastic smirk. "I've led one helluva charmed life."

Another long pause and then...

"Thank you." Grady looked directly into the man's eyes and prayed he could see the sincerity behind his words.

Confused by the sentiment, Olly's dark brows gathered together. "Why are you thanking me?"

"You sacrificed your freedom for the sake of your sister. That's damn honorable. And I, for one, am grateful for what you did." He pushed past an unexpected rush of emotions. "I know your sister is, too."

The others joined in with their own supportive comments, but soon the conversation died dow, and Izzy spoke up again.

"I shared this with all of you because I wanted to make sure you understood the kind of man my brother really is. He's never been into drugs, has had no run-ins with the law, either before or after that awful night. And he sure as hell isn't in bed with Dante Valdez."

"Boss said you drive delivery trucks for him?" Jacobs brought the conversation back to their most pressing issue.

"I do." Olly nodded. "But that's not why I'm really there."

"What do you mean?" Declan inquired.

Giving his sister a sideways glance, Olly waited until Izzy gave him a nod before revealing his true motive behind getting a job with Valdez. And what the man shared surprised everyone in the room.

9

GRADY and the others gave Olly their full attention as they waited to hear the man's true motive for agreeing to work for a man as crooked as Dante Valdez.

"The last time I was in the city, I met a woman. Her name is Rose Goodwin, and at the time, she was twenty-eight. Rose and I had a lot in common...both loners. Both have records. Our relationship was purely platonic, but I grew to care about her very much."

"Where is Rose now?" Grady looked at the other man and waited.

"That's the thing. No one knows."

"You've been out of Denver, what...two years?" Declan pointed out. "Isn't it possible Rose moved away from the area like you did?"

"No." Olly shook his head with confidence. "I tracked down her best friend, who still lives here. She told me Rose was doing really well. Had her own place and was excited because she'd just gotten hired on as a hostess at some fancy Mexican restaurant here in town."

And just like that, it all came full circle.

"Let me guess." Grady shifted in his chair. "The name of the restaurant is Los Cocina."

Olly nodded. "I started asking around. Turns out, there have been half-a-dozen women, ages spanning from seventeen to thirty-four, who were employed by that same restaurant and are now missing."

"Olly also found out there are seven other young women who worked at some of Valdez's other businesses here in town who, after they were 'promoted' to a spot at the restaurant, are now also missing."

"That's why I didn't tell my sister I was back in town." The other man turned to Izzy. "I knew if I told you what I was doing, you'd want to help. And I didn't want you getting anywhere near Valdez or the people who work for him."

Couldn't agree more.

"That's it, then." Grady looked at his boss. "The restaurant has to be the key."

Standing at the front of the room, Riedell nodded, his hands resting low on his denim-clad hips. "I agree. That's where our focus needs to be." To the team he said, "Let's start poking around. See what we can find out about these missing women. Maybe we can find something down that avenue that can get us a warrant to search."

"If Valdez is using Los Cocina as a front, there has to be something there we can use."

"But the FBI already said they suspected Valdez of using the restaurant as a front for his trafficking business," Izzy pointed out. "If they haven't been able to find anything useful by now, then how—"

"The Feds are held by a much tighter leash than we are," Riedell explained.

"Not to mention, they've been looking into it as the big-picture type of investigation," Kim pointed out. "It's quite possible for them to have done a thorough investigation based on what they had available at the time."

"Kim's right." Declan nodded. "Those guys are the best at what they do, but there's just one problem…"

Following his partner's train of thought, Grady finished with, "They're Feds."

"Make sense." Riedell agreed. "People have a tendency to open up with those they view as peers, as opposed to authority figures."

"And if the employees at Los Cocina know what kind of man they're working for"—Jacobs rejoined the conversation —"they sure as hell aren't going to risk their lives by talking to the cops."

"So here's the plan moving forward." Their boss reclaimed control of the room. "We're going to begin a thorough investigation into everything related to Los Cocina. I've been on the phone all morning trying to get us a warrant to search the restaurant and any other property related to it. I'll keep working on that while the team puts boots on the ground. Dress down, conceal your weapons, and don't show your badges unless, or until, it becomes necessary. We don't want to spook these people like the Feds most likely did."

"What about Olly and me?" Izzy asked.

Turning his gaze to hers, Riedell said, "Our tech guys are going to fit your brother with a two-way wire and a camera." Sliding his attention to Olly, he added, "For now, it's business as usual. Valdez calls with a job, you take it. But keep your eyes and ears out for anything that might possibly tie Valdez to those missing girls, and/or the weapons and drugs the Feds believe he's also running through there."

"Sounds like a plan to me." Olly sat up straight and gave Riedell a tip of his chin.

"Hold on." Izzy's voice tightened with worry. "Are we sure Valdez doesn't suspect Olly of anything?" She turned her hazel gaze toward Grady, the worry there clouding her otherwise vibrant browns and greens. "After what happened last night..."

A tiny shiver ran through her, the display of fear renewing Grady's silent vow to find the bastard who took a shot at her...and end him.

"It's a valid concern," Kim chimed back in. "The shooting took place right outside Olly's apartment building. Cops were everywhere, and if the shooter stuck around, it's possible he saw the two of you getting chummy with the other officers on scene."

"But I stayed on my side of the street, just like all the other tenants in my building," Olly reminded them. "And when your boss came to my door, I made sure a few comments were audible from all the way down the hall. Just for good measure."

Grady smirked, wishing he could've been present for that little show.

Yep. Definitely like this guy.

Actually he damn well loved him.

Oliver Garcia may have been dealt a shit hand, but it's how he handled himself in the face of adversity that impressed Grady. Even as a young man—a kid, really—the guy had done whatever it took in order to save his sister from one of the worst traumas a person could experience. Not to mention the years of suffering that typically followed an attack of that nature.

And he's been paying the price ever since.

Making a mental note to do whatever he could to help Izzy's brother out once this was all over, Grady got his head back in the game and focused on the problem at hand.

"And I played it up, as well," Riedell added, also referring to his and Olly's door-to-door conversation.

"I'd say you're in the clear." Jacobs' deep voice filled the room. When the team's attention turned to him, his focus went straight to Olly. "Think about the type of guy Dante Valdez is. If he even suspected you were working with the cops, don't you think he would've acted on that shit last night?"

"Or even this morning," Kim agreed. "You slept at your place last night, yeah?" When Olly confirmed this, she began to nod. "I think Blake's right. Valdez had hours to move in after the cops cleared out last night. And correct me if I'm wrong, but didn't you have a meeting with him first thing this morning?"

"I did." Olly looked down the table to where Kim was sitting. "I've never personally witnessed the man in action, but I didn't pick up any wonky vibes this morning."

"What did you guys talk about?"

"It was just another delivery job. Me and a couple guys put a load of supplies on the truck, and then I drove them to another warehouse across town. That was it."

"You have any idea what the supplies were?"

Olly shook his head. "No clue. The containers are always sealed, and there's no way to tamper with them without it being obvious."

"So he had you meet at the ass crack of dawn to move boxes of stuff from one warehouse to the other?" Jacobs frowned. "That's it?"

"That was it."

"Could've been a loyalty test of sorts," Grady pointed out. "Just to make sure you can follow orders as they were given."

"Wouldn't put it past him. But I was around him for

about three hours, and I didn't pick up on anything out of the ordinary. And trust me, I've been around him and his men enough to know he doesn't play. You cross Valdez, you may as well start digging your own grave."

The comment sent a flash of worry across Izzy's pretty face. Without thinking, Grady reached over and covered her hand with his as a show of support.

Her surprised gaze flew up to his, but rather than pull away, she rewarded him with a tiny smile.

That's right, sweetheart. I'm here, and I always will be. For as long as you want.

Declan cleared his throat, the sound meant to remind Grady where he was and who was watching. He didn't care.

Izzy was it for him, so these guys—including Riedell— were just gonna learn how to deal with it. That being said, he also needed to keep his head in the game and stay focused on their task at hand.

For both Izzy's and Olly's sakes.

"When will you see Valdez again?" Riedell asked Olly.

"Tonight. His muscle texted me on the drive here. We're supposed to meet up at the main warehouse at eleven tonight for some sort of big job."

"He didn't give you anything more than that?"

The question came from Cole.

"That's all I got," Olly answered. "I will say, this is the first time a job has been specifically described as 'big'. But other than that, the text sounded like every other one I've gotten in the past."

"Maybe that's all we need." Grady looked at Riedell. "It's not a lot, but Olly just said they've never mentioned whether a job is big or small before. For Valdez's man to specifically say this one is big..." His gut tightened. "Boss, this could be a transport run."

For what? They had no way of knowing.

"I hear you." Riedell nodded. "Okay, so here's what we'll do. Olly, I need you to write down the address to where you're supposed to meet Valdez tonight. I'll keep working on getting a warrant, but in the meantime, I want the rest of you to plan as if we already have it in-hand. We'll get to that warehouse tonight, well before the job is supposed to take place." To Olly, he added, "You won't be able to see us, but we'll be there. But we need you to get eyes on whatever it is Valdez is transporting."

"How is he supposed to do that?" Izzy's voice was laced with doubt. "You heard what he said. If he tampers with the product, Valdez or one of his men will see."

"I'll figure it out, Sis," Olly reassured her. "It's one thing to start screwing with the stuff on my own. But if I know these guys are there, ready to have my back, I'll be more willing to risk taking a peek."

"The second you have eyes on the product, we'll need a verbal cue. Come up with something you'll remember that will signal us without giving you away."

"How about this? If I see concrete evidence against Valdez, I'll say something like... it's a good night to make money."

"I like it." Grady sent the other man a nod.

"So do I," Riedell agreed. "All right, boys and girls. Let's work the plan. I want everything in place and ready to go by nine. That gives us two hours to make sure there aren't going to be any hiccups before our guy shows up."

"What about me?" Izzy's gaze landed on Riedell's. "Is there anything I can do to help?"

"You can help by staying home and keeping yourself safe," Grady answered for his boss.

"Thorne's right." His sergeant thankfully had his back

on this. "Until we know for sure who came after you last night, we need you to continue keeping a low profile. That means going straight home from here, staying inside, and keeping your doors locked. A uniformed officer will be watching guard from outside, just like last night."

Grady could tell Izzy wanted to play a more active role in helping them, as well as protecting her brother. But he wasn't going to pretend knowing she would be at home under police protection while they were working the case didn't put his mind—and his heart—at ease.

Another thought crossed Grady's mind. To Olly, he asked, "You drive yourself here?"

"Took a ride share," the other man answered. "Didn't want to risk my car being spotted at the police station, just in case."

"Smart." Jacobs shot Olly a look of approval.

"Okay, people. We have a lot to do and not much time to do it. Let's get moving."

With that, Sgt. Riedell turned and left the room. Blake, Cole, Kim, and Declan followed suit.

"Come on, Olly." Kim flashed him a kind smile. "I'll take you to our tech guy to get you set up with the wire and mic."

"Fun times." Olly pushed himself to his feet.

As he passed by Izzy, she stood and gave her brother a long, tight hug. They shared whispered words of sibling love and another hug before Olly turned his attention to Grady.

"Thanks for keeping my sister safe last night." The other man offered his hand.

"Never have to thank me for that, Olly." Grady returned the gesture. "I'll always have her back."

The two men shared a look that said it all. Grady let him know Izzy was safe with him, and Olly reciprocated with a look of guarded trust. And in that moment, Grady knew they both had the same priority...

For Izzy to be happy and protected.

Kim and Olly left the room, leaving Grady and Izzy alone for the first time since he'd left her bed hours earlier.

"We'll be with him the whole time, Iz. First sign of danger, the team will move in, and we'll get him out of there. You have my word."

"He's not the only one I'm worried about." She moved into his personal space. "Promise me you'll be careful, too."

"Cross my heart." He made a show of drawing an invisible X over his chest.

He was rewarded with a ghost of a smile that barely reached her eyes. "I'm sorry I didn't tell you about my foster dad before sharing the story with the entire team."

"That story was yours to tell or not, in the manner you wanted. I'm just sorry you ever had to go through that."

"Olly, too." She grimaced. "He went through so much worse."

"Not worse, Iz. Different." Moving closer, Grady took one of her delicate hands in his and squeezed. "You are both survivors in your own right."

"I just hope Olly survives what he's about to do."

"Hey, come here." He pulled her into a comforting embrace. "It's going to be okay."

"You can't know that for certain."

"Sure, I do." He kissed the top of her head before pulling back to look at her directly. With a smirk, he asked, "Did I forget to mention I can see into the future?"

"Is that right?" The weight behind Izzy's hazel gaze lifted slightly. "In that case, what does that crystal ball of yours see in our future?"

"You and me?" Grady's heart gave a hard kick. "Lots of

smiles and laughter. Me spending every day showing you just how much I love you."

"And the nights?" Her voice teased of hopeful promises.

"Sex." The blurted word escaped without hesitation. "Lots and lots of sex."

Izzy laughed, the light in her eyes returning tenfold. Which had been his goal all along.

"I'll call you as soon as it's over," he promised.

"I'll keep my phone on me at all times."

The two shared a slow, sweet kiss before forcing themselves to leave the room in search of the others. When they got back out to the bullpen, they said one final goodbye before Izzy took off down the stairs to meet back up with her assigned police escort.

As for Grady, he went straight to work, preparing for what he hoped would be the end of Valdez's reign.

10

Izzy stared at her phone for what felt like the millionth time in the last twenty minutes. It was almost ten-twenty, which meant Olly should be arriving at the warehouse any time between now and eleven.

Struggling to keep her nerves at bay, she'd tried keeping herself busy by dusting, vacuuming, cleaning out her pantry and fridge. Not a single one of those things needed to be done, but she was waiting for the team's undercover op to begin, so...

I just hope Olly finds something the cops can use to take Valdez down once and for all.

Worrying about her brother had always been a daily thing for her. But now she had *two* men she loved serving on the front lines, and it was a hard pill to swallow.

But this was Grady. She'd seen him and his team in action countless times and knew first-hand what a well-oiled machine Denver's Major Crimes unit was.

They've got this, Iz. Trust them to do their jobs and keep Olly safe.

The voice in her head was right. She needed to try not to

stress and trust Grady and his team to take care of business. After all, they were the very best detectives in the city.

Those motivating thoughts had just rolled past when her phone began to ring. The sound she'd been waiting to hear nearly made her jump out of her skin. Snatching it from the kitchen table—where she'd forced herself to stop and sit in an effort to calm her nerves—Izzy nearly dropped the damn thing but managed to answer it on the second ring.

"Hello? Grady?"

"Yeah, sweetheart. It's me."

Relief had her shoulders relaxing and the breath in her lungs releasing in one, large stream of air. "Has it started? Is Olly there?"

"Olly isn't here, but we've still got about forty minutes to go-time. I just wanted to let you know the team's here and everything's set up and ready to go. We're just waiting."

Forty minutes to go-time. Right. "Sorry. I knew it wasn't time yet, I just thought..." Another sigh. "I guess I'm just really anxious."

"It's going to be okay, Iz." His deep voice rumbled. "I've got a good feeling about this one."

She nearly smiled. "Thank you for saying that."

"I need to go, but I'll call as soon as I can." There was a slight pause and then, "I love you."

Her chest warmed with emotion. "I love you, too."

It was so strange. Her entire adult life she'd refrained from letting herself get close enough to even think about uttering those words to anyone. But saying them to this man didn't feel strange at all. In fact...

It feels pretty fantastic.

But then Grady ended the call, sending her back into the land of torturous purgatory. And since her home would almost certainly pass a white-glove inspection, Izzy was forced to search for other ways to pass the time.

She read a book she wasn't really reading. She watched a show on her DVR list she knew would have to be re-watched at a later date. Even taking a long, hot bath with her favorite playlist blaring in her ears did nothing to ease the massive ball of nerves filling her very soul.

If anything, she was even *more* ramped up than before Grady had called. Because it had been nearly an hour since then, and there was still no word.

The waiting is the worst.

How many times had she heard those words? From parents of missing children to those awaiting a judge's final custodial ruling.

Victims' families who were living each day of their lives worried their loved one's killer would be set free. Or the families of police officers and other law enforcement agents who are often forced to sit on the sidelines while the brave men and women they love run head-first toward danger.

During her years as a forensic psychiatrist, Izzy had pretty much seen and heard it all. And the one thing she'd heard over and over and over...

The waiting is the worst.

She glanced at the clock again. It was eleven fifty-five. Five. More. Minutes.

It's going to be okay. Grady promised it would be okay.

The ringing of a phone startled her a second time. Sitting up on her chaise, she picked it up from the cushion beside her and frowned at the number lit up on her screen.

With a swipe of her thumb, Izzy answered her brother's unexpected call. "Olly? Why are you calling me? Aren't you supposed to be at the—"

"Get the hell out of there!"

The alarm in his frantic voice had her jumping to her feet. Pulse skyrocketing, she held the phone tightly as she tried making sense of what was going on.

"Get out? What are you talking about? What's wrong?"

"Valdez knows!" he growled, his voice sounding strained. "Ah, hell, Iz. The bastard knows everything! I-I don't know how, but..." A rough cough. "Iz, he sent Tony after me."

"The guy from your apartment?" The man who'd blindly follow Valdez straight into hell? *Oh, God.* "Olly, are you okay? Did he hurt you?"

"Just a scratch." Another cough. "Listen, you need to get out of there right fucking now. I took care of Tony, but before the fucker died, he said Valdez was headed to you."

Izzy's breath caught in her throat, her head spinning as she began to move. "Tell me where you are." She ran toward her shoes and keys. "I'm coming to get you."

"I'm on my way to you, but I don't know if I'll get to you in time." His breathing sounded labored. "Just go. Take your phone and get someplace safe. I've already called Grady, and he and his partner are on their way to you now, but I don't want you to wait. When you're sure you're safe, call Grady and tell him where to find you, and then call me. I'll meet you there."

How is this happening?

"I'm putting my shoes on now, and—"

"Forget the shoes, Iz. Get the fuck out of that house right this fucking sec—"

A loud pop reached her ears from somewhere outside. It was a sound Izzy would recognize anywhere.

Gunfire.

"Olly?" She stood in the middle of her living room, her entire body trembling with fear. "I-I think it's too late."

"What do you mean?"

"I just heard a gunshot from outside. It sounded like it came from the front, which is where I last saw my protective detail." She swallowed a giant knot of fear, her heart kicking against her ribs in a painful staccato. Lowering her voice to a whisper, Izzy told her brother, "I think Valdez is already here."

"Back door, now!"

Izzy spun on her socked feet and started for the door off her kitchen. "In case I don't make it, I need you to know I love you!"

"I love you, too, Sis. Now stop talking and get your ass out of that house!"

She was almost to the back door when it was forced open with a bang. Izzy cried out in surprise and skidded to a stop. Her stomach dropped when she came face-to-face with Dante Valdez.

Looming in her doorway, the man was the epitome of menacing. His dark hair was peppered with strands of silver, his square jaw locked down tight. But the eyes...

The evil Izzy found there turned her veins to ice.

"Izzy!"

"It's Dante Valdez," she said the man's full name so there'd be no mistake later, when her brother gave his statement to the police.

At least that way, when they find my body, there won't be any doubt.

Lowering the phone to her side, Izzy slid her phone into the front pocket of her sweater but kept the call with Olly open so he could hopefully hear. She forced herself to meet the murdering man's blood-curdling gaze.

"That was the cops," she lied to the most dangerous man she'd ever faced. "They're already on their way, but if you leave right now, you'll still have time to get away."

"Oh, I'll leave." His deep voice rasped, his accent obvious but not disruptive to the clarity of his English. "But not before I finish what I came here to do."

"Killing me will only make things worse for you, Dante." Izzy attempted to convey a sense of reasoning. "If the cops had anything concrete, you'd already be in cuffs. The fact that you're not means you can walk out that door and leave a free man."

"I know what you and your brother have been up to," Valdez spoke as if she hadn't said a word. He moved toward her with slow, purposeful steps. "Olly's already paid for betraying me. And you, Isobel, helped him. Unfortunately for you both, that's not something I can let slide."

With every step he took in her direction, Izzy took a shaky one backward. It was clear he didn't know Olly was the one she'd been speaking with, nor did the bastard realize it was *his* man who had paid for his mistakes.

Keep him talking, Iz. Buy as much time as you can.

"Didn't you hear me when you broke down my door?" Another step backward. "I was on with the nine-one-one operator when I said your name. They know you're here. They know it's you who broke into my home."

"Is that supposed to scare me?"

"It's supposed to make you realize you're about to lose everything you've worked so hard for. A business you've *killed* to protect." *Get a confession.* "Because you have killed, haven't you, Dante? You just admitted to murdering my brother tonight." Thank *God* Olly came out on top of that one. "But there's also those three Los Reyes boys the cops told me about. I believe the most recent one was named Gomez."

"Gomez had a big mouth and sticky fingers," Valdez

revealed. "It's like the old saying goes...it's not personal. It's business."

"Is that why you sent Tony Fitch to kill him?"

The man's steps faltered slightly. "Who told you that?"

"Lucky guess." Izzy forced a casual shrug. "I mean, the man is attached to your hip most days, right? He's loyal to the point he'd kill at the snap of *your* fingers. Stands to reason a job as important as a traitor would require the best you've got."

A spine-shivering smile lifted the man's lips into an evil grin.

"I heard you were smart."

"I am, which is why you should listen to what I'm telling you. Unless you want this night to be your last, I suggest you leave my home now, before it's too late."

"Told you, sweet Isobel." He continued his advance. "Once you're taken care of..."

The maniac didn't seem fazed by the fact that the cops were on their way. If Izzy's assessment of the narcissistic jerk was right, that either meant Valdez truly believed he had time to kill her and get out before the police arrived, or...

He no longer cares.

Either outcome didn't bode well for Izzy. She needed to come up with a plan, and she needed it right freaking now.

Run, Iz. It's your only option. You have to run!

As if Grady were standing right beside her, the words she could swear had come from him rang through her head. Knowing it was her only chance at survival, she decided she'd rather die fighting than to willingly give up her life to the son of a bitch still moving toward her.

She glanced over one shoulder, mentally gauging the distance between her and the front door. There was about ten feet she needed to cover, but if she moved fast enough...

Izzy whirled around and ran as fast as her legs would take her. For a second, she thought she might actually have a chance to get outside before Valdez could catch her.

She made it halfway to the door when he slammed his body into hers from behind.

The carpeted floor sped toward her as she and Valdez fell to the ground with a thud. The air was forced from her lungs, and Izzy struggled to catch her breath while also fighting against the man currently sprawled on top of her.

In one swift move, Valdez flipped her entire body over before straddling her with his heavy form. The man's meaty hands held both wrists in place so tightly, she actually worried her bones would break.

"You should've stayed in your lane, shrink. You have no business being in my world."

"Let me go!" She turned and twisted against his painful grip.

But Valdez simply laughed.

Moving her wrists together, he held them in one fist while using his free hand to pull a large, shiny knife from his waistband. Izzy whimpered, then silently berated herself for showing this bastard a single second of fear.

She was going to die soon. That was no longer a question. But *how* she died...

I won't be a victim. Not again. Never. Fucking. Again.

With renewed strength, Izzy continued to buck and kick her legs, doing her best to cause as much pain to her attacker as she could. But her efforts were in vain.

Valdez was too big and too strong.

He put the knife to the edge of her throat, the paper-thin point piercing her skin on contact. Izzy froze, her breath held unmoving in her stuttered lungs for fear she'd cause the blade to cut her even more. A tear escaped the corner of her eye, the warm droplet falling across her temple before landing on the carpet below. But she refused to beg.

I'm sorry Olly. So, so sorry. And Grady...God, I loved you so much. More than you will ever know. Please go on. Be happy. You both deserve to be happy.

Another tear slipped from the corner of her eye, the warm droplet falling across her temple before landing on the carpet below. But she refused to beg.

Knowing her time on this earth had come to an end, Izzy chose to go out with as much dignity as she could. With her gaze locked on the man hell-bent on ending her life, she kept her chin steady and dared him to get on with it.

"What are you waiting for?" she demanded carefully, making sure to only move her lips. "You came here to kill me, so just do it. Slice my throat and be done with it."

In an unexpected move, Valdez pulled the blade a few centimeters away and smiled. "You surprise me, Isobel. I expected you to beg. Most people do, you know."

"I'm not most people."

"No." He chuckled. "I don't suppose you are. It's a shame, really. My buyers would've paid top dollar for a piece of ass like you."

Remembering the phone in her pocket, Izzy prayed whoever was listening could hear the conversation clearly enough to understand what she was doing.

"How much you thinking?" She goaded the man to share more details about his sex trafficking ties. "What did all those other women bring in? A grand? Five?"

"Try fifty," Valdez sounded offended. "The women I sell aren't the pieces of shit I could pick off the streets. I run the most successful trafficking business in the tri-state area. I've made millions off the girls I've sold. And I'll make even more after you're gone."

Just then, a shadow fell over the wall behind Valdez. Izzy saw it, knew exactly what had created it. Valdez, however, was too busy bragging about his illegal dealings to notice.

"What about the drugs and guns?" She did her best to keep him talking. "Those bring in millions, too?"

"More money that you could count in a lifetime. Now as much as I'd love to spend more time with you, I have other places to be. And, as you so generously pointed out, the cops are headed this way, so—"

"We're already here, asshole."

Yes!

Grady's imposing form came into view behind Valdez, his department-issued weapon pressed against the back of Dante's head. Standing beside him with his gun drawn, the barrel pointed at Valdez, was Declan.

"Drop the knife and stand up slowly." Grady's voice was low. Deadly.

And the way he was staring at Valdez...

He wants to do it. He wants to pull the trigger.

Izzy didn't want that for him. She didn't want to be the cause of the black mark killing another human could leave. Not even a man intent on killing her.

But rather than follow Grady's directions, Valdez put the blade back to her throat and smirked. "How about you drop your gun, and I don't slice her ear-to-ear?"

"I won't ask you again."

Valdez stared down at her, the look in his eyes telling. A man like that would rather die than go to prison. And even in death, he'd want to keep his reputation intact, which meant only one thing...

He's going to do it. He's going to kill me.

Izzy knew this was her final chance. If she died fighting, so be it.

"I love you, Grady." Her declaration came out slow and precise. When those heart-stealing eyes slid to hers, she willed him to understand her unspoken plan. "I love you, and...I trust you."

A muscle in his left cheek twitched as Izzy held her breath and began a silent countdown starting at five. When she got to one, she shot up one final prayer and swung her head as far to the right as she could.

The sharp sting from the knife registered as it cut into her skin. A fraction of a second later, a deafening bang filled the room.

She expected to feel Valdez's lifeless body fall on top of hers. Before that could happen, he was unceremoniously pulled off her and tossed to the side by the man who'd just ended his life...

And saved hers.

"Izzy!"

"Grady!"

He pulled her to her feet and swallowed her whole in his warm embrace. Their frantic hearts beat together as one, and it was in that moment Izzy knew this man was her future.

"Are you all right?" His hands rushed in their efforts to search for possible injuries. "Did he hurt you?" His worried gaze turned to stone as it fell on her tender neck. "He cut you."

"It's nothing." Izzy put a hand to her tender skin. Her fingers met with something warm and sticky.

Beside them, Declan cuffed Valdez's corpse as per procedure before getting on his police radio to report the night's terrifying events.

"It's not nothing. You're fucking bleeding." Grady growled, pulling her hand away to inspect the damage

Valdez's knife had caused. But then, "It doesn't look too deep, but you're still going to the hospital to get checked out by a doctor."

"Not until I see Olly." It was then that Izzy remembered her phone. Reaching into her pocket, Izzy retrieved her phone and put it to her ear. "Olly? Are you still there?"

"I'm here."

There was an echo that hadn't been there before. Almost as if his voice were in stereo. When her brother's face came into view from behind where Grady stood, she understood why.

"Olly!" She ran to her brother and threw her arms around him.

"Hey, Sis." Olly grunted from the unexpected impact. "Take it easy, would ya?"

Remembering his strained voice and that he sounded as though he was in pain, Izzy took a step back to give her brother an assessing glance. She spotted the blood instantly.

"You've been shot?"

"It's nothing," he repeated the words she'd just offered Grady. "Bullet only grazed me."

Her eyes lowered to the gash cutting across her brother's left bicep. Seeing for herself that there were no other injuries, she pulled him in for another hug.

"You're really okay." She gave him a tight squeeze.

Hugging her back, Olly kissed the top of her head and said, "We *both* are."

"I appreciate the heads up, Garcia." Grady joined them with an outstretched hand.

Her brother released her to shake the hand of the man she loved. "Appreciate you hauling ass to get to my sister in time."

"It wasn't an option." The man *she* loved stared straight

into her brother's hazel eyes. "I love your sister, Oliver. And I plan to marry her."

"You do?" Izzy felt her eyes grow wide.

"I do." Grady turned that soul-searching gaze to hers. "When you're ready."

Now. I'm ready now.

A month ago—hell, a week ago—the mere idea of weddings and marriage would've sent her running for the hills. But not anymore.

In the distance, sirens made themselves known. The peeling sound growing louder with each second that passed. As if he'd forgotten all about the other two men in the room—and the dead body lying less than a handful of feet from where they stood—Grady pulled her back into the warmth and safety of his strong embrace.

"I thought I lost you." He pressed his lips to hers. "I was so scared I wouldn't get to you in time."

"I'm not going anywhere." She kissed him back. "Not without you by my side."

"You are constantly surprising me, Dr. Garcia."

"Oh, trust me, Detective." Izzy curved her lips into a mischievous smile. With her breath feathering against his lips, she whispered, "You ain't seen nothin' yet."

PRE-ORDER MARKED FOR DISASTER, THE NEXT EXCITING STORY IN ANNA BLAKELY'S BESTSELLING MARKED SERIES NOW:

HTTPS://AMZN.TO/3V7XMUT

Former Navy SEAL Ivan Petrov is accustomed to a life of adrenaline and secrecy. No longer under Uncle Sam's thumb, he now works for Denver's most renowned nightclub owner and private investigator. But when his boss and his new wife depart for their honeymoon, Ivan is left in charge of the club, plunging him into a situation he never expected.

Cera Davidson is on the run from a deranged stalker. Desperately seeking a safe haven, she goes in search of the owner of Sin, the city's hottest nightclub. But the face she meets isn't the one she expects. With her choices—and time—running out, Cera reluctantly agrees to place her life in Ivan's hands. A decision that will forever change the course of both their futures.

Brought together by fate, these two strangers soon become so much more. However, just when they believe they have eluded the clutches of danger, disaster strikes with deadly consequences, threatening not only their lives but also the lives of everyone in Denver.

In this gripping tale of suspense, passion, and resilience, Anna Blakely weaves a web of intrigue that will leave readers breathless until the very last page. Ivan and Cera's journey is a testament to the power of love and the strength of the human spirit when faced with unimaginable danger.

***MARKED FOR DISASTER is Book 6 in Anna's Marked Series and will contain a full, compete story with a Happy Ever After and no cliffhangers.

ALSO BY ANNA BLAKELY

MARKED SERIES

Marked For Death
Marked for Revenge
Marked for Deception
Marked for Obsession
Marked for Disaster

R.I.S.C. SERIES
TAKING A RISK, PART ONE

Taking a Risk, Part Two
Beautiful Risk
Intentional Risk
Unpredictable Risk
Ultimate Risk
Targeted Risk
Savage Risk
Undeniable Risk
His Greatest Risk

BRAVO TEAM SERIES
RESCUING GRACELYNN

Rescuing Katherine
Rescuing Gabriella
Rescuing Ellena
Rescuing Jenna

Charlie Team Series
Kellan
Greyson
Asher
Rhys
Parker

TAC-OPS SERIES
GARRETT'S DESTINY

Etthan's Obsession

WANT TO CONNECT WITH ANNA?

Newsletter signup (with FREE Bravo Team prequel novella!)
BookHip.com/ZLMKFT
Join Anna's Reader Group: www.facebook.com/groups/blakelysbunch/
BookBub: https://www.bookbub.com/authors/anna-blakely
Amazon: amazon.com/author/annablakely
Author Page: https://www.facebook.com/annablakelyromance
Instagram: https://instagram.com/annablakely
Twitter: @ablakelyauthor
Goodreads: https://www.goodreads.com/author/show/18650841.Anna_Blakely

Made in United States
Troutdale, OR
07/02/2023